P9-AQE-553

HIS VOICE WAS LIKE A HONEYED CARESS. . . .

There was a brief second when Maile thought she could escape him, but then his lips were touching hers, and she was too stunned by the feelings fluttering inside her to do more than stand there frozen, letting him take what he wanted.

"No!" she cried, as she felt herself flooding with treacherous warmth . . . as his kiss deepened and her senses reeled. . . .

CANDLELIGHT ECSTASY ROMANCES™

THE DEVIL'S PLAYGROUND

JoAnna Brandon

A CANDLELIGHT ECSTASY ROMANCE™

Published by
Dell Publishing Co., Inc.
1 Dag Hammarskjold Plaza
New York, New York 10017

Dell ® TM 681510, Dell Publishing Co., Inc.

Candlelight Ecstasy Romance™ is a trademark of
Dell Publishing Co., Inc., New York, New York.

ISBN: 0-440-11985-5

Printed in the United States of America
First printing—July 1982

Dear Reader:

In response to your continued enthusiasm for Candlelight Ecstasy Romances™, we are increasing the number of new titles from four to six per month.

We are delighted to present sensuous novels set in America, depicting modern American men and women as they confront the provocative problems of modern relationships.

Throughout the history of the Candlelight line, Dell has tried to maintain a high standard of excellence, to give you the finest in reading enjoyment. That is now and will remain our most ardent ambition.

Anne Gisonny
Editor
Candlelight Romances

CHAPTER 1

"You cannot spend your entire life being a coward," Mike Sloan had told her. He said it teasingly when Maile Riordan had declined his invitation to go a few laps the day they met at his speedway. And he said it again a week before his car went into the wall, killing him.

"And you cannot hide from life." He seemed to be right there, urging her to do what she had come here to do, mainly to exorcise his ghost. With a sigh Maile left her car parked by the gate and started to walk around the track—a woman of average height, boyishly slim, with thick black hair that was hanging carelessly about her slender shoulders.

In her mind Maile could hear the crowds cheering, although the bleachers were empty. She heard the rumbling of engines and instinctively scrambled toward the fence for safety, but when she glanced over her shoulder, the oval track was empty. Shaking her head at her fancifulness, she expelled her breath in a sigh. There was no one there, no green car with a broad yellow stripe coming at her at a reckless speed. And there would never again be that sandy-haired man with the twinkling blue eyes to jump out of the car, laughing because he had come too close to her and made her scurry away. The entire speedway was deserted except for her and a calico cat that was rummaging through a trash bin.

The wind was rising, dredging up odds and ends from beneath the bleachers and assailing her with them. Maile squeezed her eyes shut to ward off the dust the wind had raised, then reached up a hand to wipe her face and was surprised to find tears on her cheeks. She sniffed. There was no sense in crying. Mike was gone, and no amount of tears would bring him back. Besides, she reminded herself with a wry twist to her lips, Mike hated crybabies.

"And now *this*," she murmured, coming to a standstill and surveying the speedway with bewildered green eyes. What in the world was she going to do with this thing Mike had left to her? He'd been crazy to entrust her with it; she knew next to nothing about operating a speedway.

Kicking an empty can out of the way as she resumed her walk, she thought about Mike and what they had meant to each other. He'd been good for her, and she had added a little quiet sanity to his fast life. She was able to smile when she conjured up his image, and found that even his ghost was laughing at her. Minnie Mouse, he'd called her; she was always scurrying here and there, always looking over her shoulder, darting from what he referred to as "the real life," always afraid to live. But never afraid to love. They had been very much in love with each other, and she had beautiful memories of their four years together that even death could not take from her.

She quickened her step, her eyes skimming over the

10

posters on the wall, the bits and pieces of paper being scattered over the track, the cat still scrounging for something to eat. She did not see or hear the car that came in through the gate and parked beside hers, and she glanced up with a start when a crisp masculine voice called out to her.

"I beg your pardon?" Green eyes that had been misting as memories of other visits to this track replayed in her mind were lifted in the direction of that voice.

Vivid blue eyes peered intently at her from beneath a fringe of eyebrows that were as dark as the man's thick wavy hair. Narrowed speculatively, they swept over her slim figure, lingering briefly on the rise and fall of her breasts beneath a black turtleneck shell. She had seen a light of admiration glimmer briefly in his eyes, but it flitted away as they roamed down to her tiny waist and farther, over her narrow hips and legs, their shapeliness obscured by the flared legs of her jeans.

"I thought to find my nephew here, with you," he said, flashing her a brief smile she suspected was forced. He had sensually full lips, and nice white teeth that contrasted beautifully with his dark golden tan.

Maile smiled, her green eyes silently framing a question. Her smile was not returned, and when he offered no explanation that would throw light on his obviously missing nephew and his reason for being there, Maile felt her own smile fading. There was no hint of warmth in the face that towered above her; only a look of extreme annoyance that detracted from the man's rugged good looks.

"As you can see, I'm the only one here." She darted a look at the gate, belatedly wishing she had thought to lock it. But how could she have anticipated that someone would come even though the sign out on the highway clearly stated that the speedway was closed until further notice.

He glanced down at her, and for a moment Maile thought he would smile, but he frowned. "I can see that for myself, Miss . . . ?"

"Yes, I'm sure you can," she returned, her voice quiet. She deliberately did not volunteer her name. She had not asked him for his name, after all. Shrugging uneasily as he stood there glowering at her, she started to walk away when she heard him speak again, to himself.

"He's very young," he murmured, eyes roaming over the speedway as though he were directing himself to it. "Too damn young to know what he wants, and I'm certainly not going to let him settle for *this*!" His features hardened angrily. "No, by God!" Swinging sharply on his heel, he strode across the track to the bleachers.

He's crazy, Maile thought bemusedly. No one functioning on all eight cylinders would behave so irrationally. But he intrigued her, and so she postponed her walk in favor of watching him.

He stood very straight, very stiff, looking at the bleachers; he reminded Maile of the papier-mâché Indian a friend of hers had standing just inside the door of her store in Tonopah, Nevada. While Maile was wondering how to get him off her property without admitting who she was, he moved up to the top bleacher and, shading his eyes against a nonexistent sun, stared at the road leading down to the speedway. After a while he turned, surveying the entire area through narrowed eyes, his expression clearly showing his intense dislike for the speedway. Maile felt certain if he could make it disappear with a snap of his fingers, he would.

12

"Is this damn place open to the public?" he called out in a rich, though distinctly annoyed, baritone.

"The gate's open, isn't it?" she shot back at him.

He glanced over his shoulder again, frowning over the empty road. Now, with his eyes not boring down on her, Maile stared at him and speculated on his identity. He was handsome, about her brother Bryan's age, but in better physical form. He had an outdoorsy look about him that his expensive clothes could not hide. As though suddenly feeling her eyes on him, he turned and caught her staring. Blushing, she quickly turned away from his cynically curved mouth.

"I don't think he's going to show. He knows I'm looking for him, but if he does—" He broke off abruptly, flicking his eyes impatiently over her. "Oh, hell! You wouldn't send him away even if I asked you."

Probably not, if I knew who the hell you were talking about. Without replying, Maile turned her back to him and resumed her nostalgic walk around the track. She heard him start his car, heard the angry slam of the door, then the tires squealing as he spun away from her car. Maile turned to see him drive out of the gate.

"Who is he, I wonder?" Probably a frustrated racer who hadn't made the grade. Why else would he show such an open dislike for Mike's speedway?

Shaking off the disturbing feeling the man had left her with, Maile resumed her solitary appraisal of her new property.

"Oh, rats!" she muttered disgustedly. She had spied a whirlwind of dust coming toward the speedway, warning her that yet another interruption was imminent. The speed at which the car was traveling reminded her of her earlier visitor.

13

Leaning against her car, she folded her arms across her breast, and waited for the sleek red Ferrari to come through the gate. If her earlier reticence had not discouraged the man, she would quickly verbalize her annoyance in having her peaceful Sunday disrupted by uncles who could not keep track of their young nephews.

But instead of the sports car, she saw a green car with a broad yellow stripe stopping beside her. Her breath constricted, and she went weak in the knees when she saw a tawny-haired man climb out of the car and come toward her. For a moment it seemed that Mike had come back to her.

She sighed wistfully. Here must be the errant nephew, she thought distractedly, eyeing the new arrival, a shrewd gleam in her eyes.

The boy smiled wide—his straight white teeth were startling against the berry-brown tan of his skin: a tall broad-shouldered boy with the sleek good looks that seemed to bear the California stamp on them. His hair, slightly too long, was whipped about his lean face by the wind. A hand, long and slender, was lifted to brush back the tawny strands that flew across his wide brow.

"Hi! You work here?" A huge smile curved his mouth as his eyes skimmed over her. "Or are you like me, sneaking in here for a last run before they close 'er up?" Brown eyes flecked with gold slid over her at a more leisurely pace, boldly assessing her.

"I understand that they are thinking of closing the speedway down for good because the owner was killed here," he continued softly, sweeping the entire speedway with a quick glance. "It's a damn shame too. I don't think Mike would've wanted to see it shut down."

"You don't think so?" Maile's voice was a barely audi-

14

ble whisper that had slid past a lump of sadness in her throat. The boy had referred to Mike with the familiarity of a longtime friend. She looked up at his face, studying his features keenly, nagging her brain to recall if she'd ever seen him before. She hadn't.

"I suppose if the speedway belonged to you, you'd open it next Sunday and invite everyone in for a free run?" She glanced up at him as she spoke, hoping he would give her an honest answer. She was still not certain what she ought to do with Mike's speedway.

He smiled diffidently. "Well, not exactly. I mean, I wouldn't let 'em come in here and use the facilities for free, but yes, I would open it on Sunday, or as soon as the weather permitted. Like I said, I don't think Mike would've wanted to see his speedway closed. He put too much time and money into it . . . and he—"

"You seem to know a lot about him," Maile interjected before the boy could say that Mike had even given his life for the track. Mike had been testing the newly graded track when his car had hit a deep rut only camouflaged by the resurfacing, and gone into the fence.

"Were you a friend of his?" A stirring of self-pity made itself felt deep within her, and she turned away from the boy's direct gaze. Mike was gone now; she should not feel this hurt that was rooted in envy, because Mike's racing friends had always seen more of him than she.

"Not really," he admitted with a sheepish grin. "I used to hang around here on the off chance that I would get to meet all the pros that came to see Mike. I met Mike one Sunday and he took me around in his car." Smiling proudly, he admitted that his biggest thrill had been when Mike had autographed his Parnelli Jones book on racing.

15

Maile smiled. Mike had been a sweet man who happily complied with whatever request was made of him.

"He gave me a pass that sort of allowed me freedom of the track." The boy smiled down at her. "I suppose he gave you one too?" His expression told her he had no doubt Mike had given her a pass not only to the track but also to Mike Sloan himself.

Blushing faintly, Maile nodded, silently agreeing that Mike had given her free access to his private life—provided she didn't mind sharing him with the track.

"Well, he sort of promised that later I could come and use the track myself but then he—"

—went off and got himself killed, she finished in her mind sadly. She breathed in deeply to ease the sudden pain that tightened her breast, knotted inside her like a clenched fist. "When did he 'sort of' promise that you could use the track?" she asked after she could trust her voice to not show the tremor that she felt inside her body.

"The week before his . . . accident." He looked down at her, his eyes intense with an expression that Maile could not understand. "I sure miss the guy," he said with a shrug of his shoulders. "He was the only one who didn't treat me like a know-nothing kid," he added wistfully. His eyes searched the posters lining the fence, his expression grave.

"Are you thinking to become a racer?"

A strange expression flickered briefly across his youthful features, and it seemed to her that his whole body stiffened with anger. "I don't really know." He started walking, his hands clenched and deep in the pockets of his jeans.

"I just want the chance to discover for myself if this is really what I want. Is that so wrong?" he demanded sharply, turning, glaring down at her as though he expected an argument from her.

Maile started. "Of course not. Who says it is?"

"My— One of my relatives," he muttered, a dark frown drawing his brown brows together above his straight narrow nose.

An uncle, no doubt. Maile frowned with annoyance, suspecting this boy was the one that that haughty man had been hoping to waylay here.

She did not ask his name, nor he hers, but somehow names did not seem all that important. He opened up to her, talking as though they were longtime friends. Maile listened quietly, adding a few comments now and then when he seemed to expect a response from her. But for the most part she listened attentively, suspecting that this was all the boy needed at the moment.

"I understand the speedway is going to be closed until May," she offered guardedly during a pause in his talk. "Why don't you call Jim Boyden, Sloan's lawyer in San Francisco, and ask for permission to come use the track on Sundays. I understand he has, uh, power of attorney." She grasped at the first words that came into her mind as he turned to look at her, a question forming on his lips. "While he—Sloan, that is—was away, Boyden took care of all his business, so he's always had a say in running the speedway."

His expression brightened. "Do you know this guy? Personally, I mean?" When she nodded, he added, "Then do you think you could put in a good word for me? I promise to be very, very careful when I'm here."

Debating only a moment, Maile nodded. There was nothing wrong, after all, she reasoned, in fulfilling Mike's wishes, and she had no doubt that Mike had given the boy permission to use the speedway. She'd call Jim in the morning, and remind him, too, not to tell the boy—or anyone else, for that matter—that she was now the owner of the speedway.

"Thanks." He looked around the speedway with a wide smile curving his lips, his joyful expression telling Maile that mentally he was already doing laps and pacing himself. She looked back at his car and cringed. If only he had not chosen Mike's colors for his own. . . .

"Do you think anyone would mind if I did a few laps right now?" His tone was hoarse with youthful eagerness he did not even try to suppress. Maile smiled and shook her head.

"There's no one here but you and me, and I won't tell if you don't." She frowned slightly, suddenly realizing she would have to stay here longer than she had at first intended. But then . . . maybe this would be the only time he could use the track, so why not let him enjoy himself?

The little-boy grin he gave her put a certain glow in his golden eyes and reinforced Maile's decision to let him run around the track. "Wow!" Letting loose a loud rebel yell, he ran back to where he had left his car.

"By the way, my name's David. What's yours?" he yelled, half turning as he started to climb into his car.

"Maile," she called back, then waved him off and went up to the bleachers. For the next forty-five minutes she was his cheering section. And though she was no expert on racing, she liked the way the boy handled himself on the track. He was controlled, yet confident and very professional in all his maneuvers.

"That was very good," she said when he finally stopped and came to join her on the bleachers.

"Was I?" He grinned proudly, showing all his teeth. He

18

removed his helmet, took a handkerchief from the back pocket of his jeans and wiped the sweat from his brow. Stuffing the linen back in his pocket, he sat down beside her, propping his green and yellow helmet on his knee.

They sat in companionable silence for a few moments, both looking out over the empty track. Then he turned and startled her by taking up her hand.

"Maile," he whispered. "A pretty name for a lovely lady." He smiled into her confused expression. "Would you consider me too fresh if I invited you out for a cup of coffee or something?"

Maile had it on the tip of her tongue to tell him that she couldn't, that she was expected at home. But then she remembered she had had only a cup of coffee before coming out to the track.

"Or something," she teased, adding she would go with him only if they went dutch treat.

David's expression went sour. "I'll respect your wish to pay your own way, Maile, but I *can* afford to take you to lunch." A muscle worked at his jaw, and she had the distinct impression that she had bruised his male ego. Her heart softened toward him.

"I'm alone in Watsonville today, and I really would enjoy having company for lunch, Maile." The intense look in his eyes embarrassed her. To veil her discomfort Maile turned to look at his car, then asked abruptly, "What kind of engine have you in that thing?"

"Three-fifty LT-one off-road Chevy," he replied with a touch of male pride in his tone, a faint smile curving his lips.

"And you can still afford to treat me to lunch?" Maile teased, rising to her feet.

He chuckled. "Only if you don't overeat."

As she drove ahead of him in her maroon Daytona Charger—a gift from Mike—Maile wondered at her hesitancy to let David know she owned the speedway. She felt a little guilty for being so secretive, but shook the feeling away, rationalizing that he had not asked who she was and she, after all, had never been one to volunteer information.

Strangely she felt at peace for the first time in months, and she credited this almost happy state of being to the boy who had accidentally lifted her out of the doldrums with his exuberance. Even if he *was* that disturbing man's nephew—and she sincerely hoped that he wasn't—she liked the boy. No, he can't be related to that obnoxious man, she thought, a disdainful twist to her wide, rather sensuously full mouth. David was warm, friendly . . . his smile sincere. And he didn't seem at all the "know-nothing kid" someone was trying to make him feel that he was.

Back at her house about an hour later Maile threw off her clothes in anticipation of immersing her tired body in a hot, bubbly bath; carelessly threw on her fluffy green robe; and sat at the kitchen table with a glass of white wine and her accounts books.

She owned a small boutique in Santa Cruz that catered almost exclusively to tourists, although a select few Bay Area residents patronized it. She'd been lucky to have the shop when Mike's death had shattered her world. She used it as therapy, hiding her sorrows in long hours of furious mental activity, filling all her empty time with hard work to keep from sinking into the black, bottomless pit of despair that had seemed to beckon to her. And she had created some of her best designs, delighting her patrons, building a name for herself—until she had achieved the dream she had shared with Mike. She was now in the enviable position of having her designs in demand by several fashion houses. A lot of the credit went to Janey Apella, her good friend and valuable employee, who had given unstintingly of her time, diligently fashioning the one-of-a-kind items that Maile designed—skirts, lounging ensembles, gowns, blouses, jeans, and sundresses—until Belle Mode was a name well-known and respected throughout the country.

Maile had a frustrating moment when she could not account for two hundred dollars withdrawn without explanation. And then she remembered making a personal loan to her brother, Bryan. Sighing wearily, she recorded the amount under MISCELLANEOUS EXPENSES. Curiously she ran her eyes over the totals and decided that she needed to have a serious talk with him. For the past year, that darned miscellaneous expenses column had increased steadily, and Bryan was the main cause of its frequent entries.

After she had finally brought the posting up to date, she closed the journal and put it away. She stretched, rotating her head to ease the tension from her shoulders. A bath. A nice, hot bath would dispel her weariness, and she might even feel good enough to call Bryan and demand to know why he had stood her up this morning.

Glancing disdainfully at the phone, Maile hurried into the bathroom and turned on the hot water in the tub, full blast. Easing herself out of her robe, she allowed it to fall around her feet.

The telephone rang. For a moment Maile debated about not answering it. Forcing herself to leave the bathroom after casting a longing glance at her hot bath, she walked resolutely to the phone and picked it up.

"Hello, Maile." Bryan's voice was strangely subdued.

"Bry. . . . Anything wrong?" She frowned. The last few weeks he'd seemed distant, preoccupied.

"I'm calling from Rick's. Why don't you come down to the speedway? After, we can go have a cup of coffee. I need to talk to you about something."

There *was* something wrong. She could tell by the underlying weariness in his tone. But she wasted no time in quizzing him on the phone. "Give me five minutes, Bry, then I'll meet you." She tried to lighten her own mood by teasing, "But you're not going to get off with just buying me coffee, Bry. You stood me up this morning, so now you have to take me out to dinner to make up for the breakfast I missed."

"You're on." He chuckled humorlessly.

Maile slipped on a plaid skirt and pink silk blouse. Forgotten was the little makeup she normally wore, the nylons she'd washed this morning, the careful fixing of her hair. She had to be satisfied with running a quick brush through her hair. Thank goodness it's only Bryan I'm going to meet, she thought, grabbing her purse and keys from the kitchen table and running out of the house.

Ten minutes later she was at the speedway and demanding to know exactly what was going on. "And don't try to evade the issue like you always do, Bry. Just come on out with it, *now.*"

"Out with what?" The haunted look in his eyes belied his casual tone, and she felt a resurgence of the unease that had gripped her when he had called her late last night and asked her to meet him at the speedway this morning— only to stand her up. He turned away from her, and Maile saw he had lost weight; his cheeks seemed too hollow.

"Dammit, Bryan, I'm not a child! There's something bothering you, has been for a long time."

"Does there have to be something wrong with *me*?" he countered, managing a brief, rather tight little smile. "Couldn't it be that I've been worried sick about you?"

Maile shook her head in silent denial but did not press the issue. Bryan was devilishly obstinate; he would tell her what was bothering him in his own sweet time, or not at all.

She'd give him time, she decided as she started away. She walked toward the bleachers, speculating on what could be bothering him. It had to be personal, for Bryan never seemed to worry about his job. He was exceptionally good at what he did and had received several cash awards for time-saving suggestions, as well as commendations for his conscientiousness. He was head accountant for the Weston Development and Investment Corporation in San Francisco. He had a good working relationship with all the employees, and with Charles Weston, the head of the corporation who seemed to like him personally.

Maile's glance slid to his solitary figure by the gate, then to his car, and she smiled amusedly. No flare, no flash— that was Bryan and his brown Mustang. A typical accountant, she mused as she ran an appraising eye over his brown-suited frame.

Since the death of their parents when Maile was twelve, they had had only each other to rely on, for the turmoil in Ireland had decimated the Riordan family, and those who remained had more important things to worry them than the welfare of the two Riordans living in the States. Or, more precisely, as her Irish cousins liked to call it, the land of milk and honey—California.

Bryan had been her only friend and confidant during those awful teen years when she was trying to discover the real Maile Riordan. When the boys had started to swarm

23

around her, trying to push her into immature but painful relationships, it was Bryan she had run to, and he had made her see that *she* had to think it was right before she should enter into any kind of relationship with a man.

They'd had only one really serious falling out, when Mike Sloan had breezed into her life. Bryan had warned her that Mike was not right for her. Mike was boisterous, fun-loving, an extrovert who loved simply everybody and was at his best when surrounded by people like himself; Maile was a loner, content with only one or two close friends.

After Maile had refused to stop seeing Mike, Bryan had not spoken to her for days, and though they were both plainly miserable, both were too stubborn to call a truce. Thanks to Mike's intervention, they had become friends again. Only in the past few weeks had Maile noticed the return of a strained relationship between them.

We're good friends, not just brother and sister, she thought as Bryan joined her on the bleachers.

Deepening shadows gathered as they sat together, not speaking for a few moments. Maile's eyes peered through the darkness to what had once been her favorite poster— Mike's car balancing on both left wheels.

"Why do they do it, Maile, do you really know?" Bryan's softly uttered question broke into her thoughts, tearing her away from the beginnings of a pleasant dream.

Knowing he was referring to the men and boys who crowd the tracks all over the world, Maile smiled. "I don't really know, Bry. For Mike, at least, it was a feeling he got when he could beat his own time. I suppose it's a combination of many things. Mostly I think it's a desire to excel, to be *número uno* at something they enjoy." She eased herself back against the upper bench, and let her thoughts wander.

A sigh escaping Bryan's tightly pursed lips brought her sharply upright. Something is definitely wrong, she thought, eyeing him worriedly.

"Why won't you tell me what's wrong?" She placed a hand on his arm, gently squeezing it under the brown sleeve.

"I don't know exactly where to begin, honey," he replied, his tone depressed, flat.

"Start at the beginning, Bry," she suggested gently. "That's usually the best place."

"It's bad, Maile."

Maile sucked in a quick breath. "You're not ill, are you, Bryan?" No, he couldn't be. He was all she had left. Nothing could happen to him! She wouldn't let it. Her fingers dug into his arm in panic, and, wincing slightly, he reached up and pried them loose.

"No, honey, I'm not ill. It's—well, with the old man gone, the son—" He stopped abruptly, turning to peer curiously at Maile after hearing her gasp. "Oh, Lord, I forgot! You didn't know that Charles Weston died."

"When did he die? And why didn't you tell me before?" Her tone was mildly reproving, inviting a short laugh from him.

"You were too wrapped up in your grief over Mike, Maile. I didn't want to add to it."

A strained silence fell between them. Finally Maile broke it, asking shortly, "Are you in danger of losing your job, Bryan?" She couldn't think what else would throw him into such a despondent mood.

"Worse than that, I'm afraid." He stood up and began

to pace in front of her on the lower bench. "If he has anything to say about it, I'll very likely end up in jail."

"What?!" Immediately Maile was on her feet, her heart thumping wildly in her breast. "Good God, why?" She searched his face in the dark, her panic growing at the defeated expression she found there.

"He will call it embezzlement."

With a sinking feeling in the pit of her stomach, Maile dropped abruptly to her seat, her heart beating erratically with fear. "*He*, Bryan? Who?" Anger edged her voice. "You're not making any sense!"

"No, I guess not. But it's because none of it makes any sense to me, Maile." His hands started to tremble, and he quickly doubled them, stuffing them impatiently into his pockets. Maile reached out her hands to him, but he shook his head at her and resumed his pacing.

"Mr. Weston gave me verbal authorization to shift several thousand dollars from one account to another. I didn't want to argue with him, since he had not been feeling well, so I merely asked him to write me a note, just to keep things legal. He agreed to, and went back to his office, presumably to write that note. Then his secretary came into it, and pretty soon the whole affair had gotten too confusing for him, and he just took off to play golf.

"The secretary came to me after a while and said that Mr. Weston had already authorized the transfer, and I should go ahead with it. She promised I'd get that note the very next morning." He shook his head as though he still found it hard to believe what had happened to him.

"Go on."

"Like an idiot, I did as the secretary said. I went ahead with the transfer." He muttered a swearword under his breath, slapping his palm against his forehead in anger. "I should have known better!" His features tightened as though he were in intolerable pain.

"What . . . happened next?" Maile choked out, her body stiff with apprehension.

"I got as far as removing the money from the business account, but it never got into his personal one. At least that's what the bank says."

Maile's hands clenched tightly on her lap, her face whitening. Even a first-year accounting student would know that removing a certain amount from one account without it showing up somewhere else in the books would smell like embezzlement. After a while she found the voice that had gone into hiding in her secret self. Fear did that to her, and she was as frightened now as she thought she would ever be.

"Is there something I can do?"

He shook his head. "Not unless you have fifty grand lying somewhere in the bottom of that," pointing to the purse that hung carelessly from her shoulder.

Had her life depended on it, Maile at that moment could not have uttered a word. Shock suspended her in a vacuum. She heard none of the night sounds around her, and she did not feel the stinging cold of the wind that was raising gooseflesh on her arms. She could not think; she could not even blink. She stared wide-eyed with reaction. This was worse than she had ever anticipated. *Fifty grand* echoed eerily in her mind. It might as well be fifty million!

She hid her face in her hands and for a moment she could think only that he was selfish in burdening her with this insurmountable problem when she was still struggling with the matter of adjusting to life without her beloved Mike.

But he was her brother. She loved him. She would never let him go to prison!

"The best I could do would be about fifteen, maybe twenty thousand if I put up my shop," she whispered. "Can you come up with the rest?" Unconsciously she crossed her fingers within the folds of her skirt, wishing he'd answer in the affirmative. After all, he had brought in a terrific salary working for Weston.

"No." Softly spoken, the word nevertheless seemed to explode inside Maile's head. "I'm flat broke."

Taking a deep breath, she tried to control the anger she felt rising inside her. She wanted to scream "What in hell do you do with all your money!" But instead, she folded her hands and while staring morosely down at her nails, asked softly, "Can't you go to this— What did you say the son's name is?"

"Jake."

"Jake. Well, can't you go to him and explain to him what happened?"

"I tried, Maile, but he won't believe me." His tone was sadly defeated. "Not that I blame him. If I were in his shoes, I probably wouldn't believe me either. It was definitely not a smart move on my part." He gave a very dry chuckle.

No, it wasn't, Maile thought sourly. Her brain danced with thoughts, but no idea merited voicing. She kept silent, feeling helpless as well as hopeless while Bryan resumed his sluggish pacing up and down the bleacher bench, his hands stuffed in his coat pockets.

Deep in thought, Maile was not aware that he had stopped pacing and was regarding her thoughtfully.

"You have *this,* Maile," he said, and she lifted her head

in time to see him give a sweep of his hand to encompass the entire speedway.

"No, Bryan!" This was her last link with Mike; she could not bear to part with it. She could not bear to part with it! The thought lodged itself comfortably in her brain, and she saw clearly that she was no longer burdened with indecision. She would keep the speedway and let Mike's friends operate it for her as they had offered to do.

"I wouldn't ask you, honey, if I had any other way. But there's no one else to turn to but you, Maile."

Sadly Maile looked around her, her eyes suddenly brimming with hot, stinging tears. If she sold the speedway, her heart would go with it. But if she did not sell, she would be literally closing the cell door behind Bryan herself, for however many years an embezzler drew in court. Her breath caught in her throat.

Oh, but she couldn't sell it! Out of desperation, a germ of an idea grew, and she grasped at it. "There's one other thing we can try. I can go see this Jake Weston and make a deal with him." She bit her full lower lip and looked down at her feet, curling her toes against the cold, thinking distractedly that she should not wear sandals in this weather.

"He cannot expect me to give up the speedway for a paltry fifty thousand," she muttered spitefully. "I'll offer him a percentage of the business."

"My God, Maile, you can't do that!" Bryan stomped his foot and glowered at her, his expression brooking no defiance. "You cannot go to him."

"And why not?" she demanded tersely.

"Because—"

A shiver ran through her body. Could it be that Bryan *had* taken that money for himself? No, he couldn't have!

29

And she should be ashamed for even thinking such a damaging thought.

"Besides, Maile, everyone says he's a cold-blooded, hard-nosed bastard. You don't know how to deal with his kind."

No, but she could learn. Before she would let go of Mike's speedway, she would learn to deal with the Devil himself. She forced a smile to lips she had bruised with her teeth, making a supreme effort to sound braver than she felt.

"I'm still going to go see him. Is he working out of his father's old office?"

"Yeah.

"And a house in Nob Hill," Bryan mocked, giving her his lopsided grin. "But you're not going *there*, m'darlin'. Aside from being an arrogant so-and-so in the business world, his reputation preceded him from Europe, and it's widely known that he's the love-'em-and-leave-'em sort."

"And you're not?" she taunted, a gurgle of amused laughter bubbling up from her chest.

He chuckled, but he neither denied her words nor defended his reluctance to commit himself to just one girl.

"Don't worry about me, Bry. I'm not looking for a man." Her eyes misted. Never. Never again would she allow herself to get so close to a man that she would want to die if she lost him. *Never!*

CHAPTER 2

Heavily draped in fog, San Francisco seemed chilly and uninviting as Maile reached its outskirts. She shivered, but it was more with apprehension than with cold. It was going to take every ounce of courage she could scrape up to face Jake Weston in his own office, and then it would take every persuasive word she had ever learned to convince him that Bryan was not a thief. She shuddered. From what Bry had told her, it was easy to imagine the man as a master puppeteer discriminately pulling strings, ruling the employees he had inherited from his father through fear rather than respect and love. Since he had refused to listen to Bryan, it seemed hardly likely that he would even see her. But she was determined to give it the old college try, for Bryan's sake. And if all else failed, she would offer him a small interest in the speedway.

She found a parking space a few blocks away from the Weston Building, and walked slowly, with a great deal of apprehension, toward the imposing gray structure. As she

31

reached its massive glass doors she had to fight down an irresistible urge to turn around and go home before she could pass through them. "If you are always going to be scared, Minnie Mouse, you might as well be dead." She could hear Mike's voice, sweetly taunting, and deadly earnest.

Sucking in a deep breath to steady herself, Maile hurried to the elevator, determined to see Jake Weston if she had to wait all day to do it.

Several hours later she thought she had. After shyly approaching the receptionist and asking if Mr. Weston could see her for a few minutes, she had been sent to one of the junior secretaries, then to another, and to another, until she had refused to go any farther.

She had met with repeated and unveiled attempts to get rid of her; she had fielded bold speculative glances; and she had perceived what might be going through the Weston employees' minds when they looked her over carefully—the women envying, the men admiring, the tailored suit she wore.

"You poor, poor dear, have you been made to wait?" asked a sweet-faced lady Maile mistook for a client of Weston's in the same fix as she. In fact, the woman was one of three executive secretaries employed by the corporation. "You come with me," she said, holding out her hand as though Maile might be a lost child in need of mothering. "I'll see to it that you see that—uh, *man*."

That tiny little pause and the unnecessary emphasis on the final word caused Maile to believe that this sweet little old lady was thinking the same thing the other secretaries were, but she was beyond caring. If it would produce Jake Weston, she was glad to let them think she had an intimate matter to discuss with him.

After seeing to it that Maile was settled in a comfortable chair in a sterile-looking office, the secretary went off, presumably to confer with her boss.

A tall thin man with graying brown hair and wearing gold-rimmed glasses that rested low on the bridge of his nose came in, and for a moment Maile took him for Jake Weston. She wondered how this man with the gaunt look could be the continental lady-killer Bryan claimed Jake Weston was. But the man turned out to be another assistant attempting to find out what she wanted with his boss. Maile politely refused to divulge her reason for wanting to see Weston, and the man went away shaking his head and mumbling to himself.

To dispel some of the nervousness that had her in its grip, Maile played a mental game with herself, watching everyone who went past the door of the office in which she was waiting, speculating on what each person did for the corporation, and how long each had worked for Charles Weston.

Her stomach made protesting sounds, and she quickly glanced around to see if anyone had heard. Maile was thankful that everyone appeared to have settled down to his or her job. She looked down at the watch pinned to her lapel and frowned. She'd already been waiting for two and a half hours. How much longer would she be made to wait?

Ten more minutes, she told herself. She would give him ten more minutes, and then she would leave. She would then write him a letter—*which is probably what I should've done in the first place,* she told herself furiously.

And then the elderly secretary returned and told her that Mr. Weston would see her. "But don't take too much of his time, dear," she cautioned. "He's a very busy man

33

with too many things to take care of at once, and not enough hours in the day to do them all, so you'll have to limit yourself to five minutes, tops." Walking briskly ahead of her, she threw open a door at the end of the long corridor and invited Maile to go in.

Briefly questioning the wisdom of this venture, Maile took a deep breath and walked into the lion's den.

Her feet sank into the plush pile of the bloodred carpet that covered the man's spacious office, but Maile hardly noticed. Her eyes were on the large paper-strewn important-looking desk in front of the windows that looked out on Montgomery Street, and the man who sat with his dark head bowed behind it. Her heart thundered in her ears as she came closer and took a better look at Jake Weston. She wished suddenly she had never come on this fool's errand because sitting behind Jake Weston's impressive desk was the wild-eyed man who had visited the speedway the day before.

"How can I help you, Miss . . . ?" The smile that had started to curve the male mouth never fulfilled its sweet promise. The blue eyes that had been narrowed over corporation papers were now wide with recognition.

"I should've known," he muttered. "Sit down and tell me what you want from me, Miss Whatever-your-name-is, but let me warn you before you waste your breath and my time. I won't hear any youthful, feminine entreaties on behalf of Arthur and his insane notions." He waved impatiently toward the straight-backed chair to the right of his desk, and dropped his eyes to his papers.

Arthur? Who the heck is Arthur? Probably his nephew. Maile shrugged. Let him battle his wayward nephew on his own time, these were *her* five minutes, and she wasn't going to waste them defending any relative of his.

"You allowed me a mere five minutes of your time, so I had better not waste any of it by making myself comfortable," Maile replied coolly. Trembling inwardly, she took a brave step toward his desk, then stepped back and gripped the back of the chair to keep those brilliant mocking eyes from seeing how badly she was shaking. That her knuckles were turning white as she gripped the chair she did not notice as she cleared her throat and began to talk.

She marveled at the coolness she heard in her voice as she unveiled her reason for coming to see him. He listened without interrupting her—for which she would be eternally grateful—leaning back in his chair, his blue eyes intent on the thin white circle on her marriage finger, left there by Mike's ring, which now lay safely tucked in her jewelry box.

"Despite what your brother must have told you to the contrary, Miss Riordan, I am not a calloused ogre. I have no real wish to send him to prison." His pause was a deliberate ruse to raise her hopes, Maile thought bitterly as he continued in a rather bored voice.

"However, I fully intend to investigate this transaction he claims my father ordered. If the results are what I suspect. . . ." He spread out his large hands, encouraging her to reach the only obvious conclusion, which infuriated her.

"But you don't understand!" she cried desperately. Her fingers were stark white, startling against the walnut grain of the chair. "Bryan would never, *never* steal from you. And he would never have done what your father asked him to do if he had not been trying to humor the old man," she finished bitterly, a disdainful expression in her overbright eyes. She sniffed, fighting back the tears of frustration she felt building up.

"At any rate," she continued in a quieter tone, "he realizes it's his fault that the money is missing, and we're prepared to repay every penny of it, if you're willing to keep the matter private between us." Her voice was strangely calm, and she could only marvel at her ability to face this scowling man without coming apart at the seams.

"I cannot do that, Miss Riordan, not if I find that he's guilty of taking the money." His voice grated in her ears, and she suspected that he had already tried and convicted her brother of embezzlement.

Eyes blazing with silent fury, Maile gritted coldly, "My brother is *not* a thief, Mr. Weston!"

"Oh?" Briefly his thick, dark eyebrows quirked mockingly, and the corners of his generous mouth twitched. "And what would *you* call a man who takes money that isn't his?"

Maile flinched. She longed to be a man for a full five minutes so that she could rearrange his arrogant features. "So you've already sat in judgment of him, found him guilty, and all that remains is for you to slam the door shut on him and rob him of several years of his life, for something he did *not* do!"

His square jawline tightened visibly. "If your brother is guilty, Miss Riordan—and notice that I say *if*—then I intend to see that he receives the punishment prescribed by law. It will have been he who closed the door upon himself when he first elected to take the money."

Blue eyes glittering angrily roamed freely over her flushed face, the smooth curves accentuated by her tight-fitting green suit. "How old are you, anyway?" he snapped. And when his demand met with cold silence, he began to speculate. "Twenty. Twenty-two at best. So why are *you* here pleading your brother's case? At his age he's certainly too old to be trying to hide behind a woman's skirts."

Maile forgot to be scared. She moved forward and leaned toward him, hands flat against the smooth surface of his desk. "Not that it's any of your business, but I'm twenty-six, Mr. Weston"—she minced her words through clenched teeth—"and I'm here simply because it's *my* speedway which we are—no, *were*—planning to use as collateral!"

For a moment Jake seemed mesmerized by the angry rise and fall of her breasts; but then he was on his feet, leaning forward, his face almost touching hers.

"A speedway?" He sucked in air noisily. "Let me tell you, *Miss Riordan,* that under no circumstances would I take a devil's playground as collateral. In my opinion they should all be shut down and racing made illegal!"

Maile blinked. Such vehemence even she could not feel, though she had lost someone very dear to her on the track. He was livid, and he frightened her. Then her fear gave way to anger, and she spat, "Thank God that you have no say over things like that. You may play at being the Almighty with those poor unfortunates who depend upon your employ for their livelihood, but I thank God that your power does not extend beyond this cushy little tower of yours where you've set yourself up as dictator!" Taking a deep breath after her outburst, she thanked him curtly for seeing her, then bade him good-bye, picked up her purse from the chair behind her, and moved toward the door.

She heard his sharp intake of breath only a moment before he was there beside her, his hands gripping her shoulders. With little effort he turned her stiff body

37

around to face him. He towered over her, even bending toward her as he was, and his eyes were glittering chips of blue ice. Maile stiffened further, calling on some inner reserve to brave the assault she feared was coming. But to her surprise it did not come. Instead, Jake seemed to suddenly wake up to what he was doing, and immediately released her.

In a deceptively gentle voice he said, "If you will spare me a little more time, we could discuss your brother's predicament, say, over lunch?"

A velvet softness had come into his eyes, but Maile did not see it. She saw only a man who held her brother's future in his cold, hard hands; a callous man who, with one word, could send an innocent man to jail.

"What else is there to discuss?" she demanded tiredly, all the fight leaving her. "You've already made up your mind that Bryan's guilty. You turned down my offer out-of-hand and—"

"I might be persuaded to reconsider, offered the proper . . . inducement," he murmured, lightly rubbing the back of his forefinger against her cheek.

Maile shuddered, understanding only too well what the devil meant. She cleared her throat; lifting her chin defiantly gave her a measure of courage. "Let's talk here," she said.

Jake's lips twitched, perhaps with amusement, perhaps with annoyance because his little ploy had not worked. "All right," he sighed, and motioned her to a chair. He walked back to his desk and sat down. Maile sat down, carefully crossing her legs at the ankle, and clasped her hands tightly in her lap.

Getting immediately to the point, "Are you willing to have me as a forty-percent partner?" he asked, watching her closely from beneath lazily lowered lashes. "A silent partner, more or less," he added softly, smiling enigmatically.

Maile almost choked. A forty-percent interest would give him a voice in the running of the speedway—or the closing of it, she thought furiously. No way! The fact was, she did not trust him even with the small interest she had thought to offer him.

"I do believe, Mr. Weston," she said, "that a fifteen-percent cut might be more equitable."

Jake's lips twitched, but he did not smile. "I beg your pardon, Miss Riordan," he retorted smoothly, "but allow me to credit your estimation of its worth with a lot of sentimental . . . attachment.

"I'll agree to stop the investigation and repay the money out of my personal accounts, if necessary, but you must agree to the forty-sixty split."

Maile forced a smile. In the first place Bryan was *not* guilty, so why would she want him to stop his miserable investigation? In the second place— "And you must allow me to suspect that you're attempting to take advantage of me simply because I'm a woman." She lifted herself out of her chair with exaggerated care.

"I know Bryan did not steal that money, Mr. Weston, and we will prove it to you somehow. But whatever happens, I will never agree to give you such a toehold in Mike's speedway. I do not trust you." Fumbling in her bag, she found her car keys and pulled them out.

He was beside her in a flash, his hand curled around her wrist. "I wonder," he said, after a moment spent looking into her angry expression, "would you be this irrational if it were you facing a jail term?" One eyebrow went up to mock her.

Maile didn't even have to consider; she replied swiftly, coldly. "If I were the one, instead of my brother, *Mister* Weston, I'd tell you to start proceedings against me and be damned!" She turned to go, only to be stopped by his firm hand closing over the fleshy part of her arm, the pressure of his grip causing her to wince. Maile glared up at him but said nothing.

"Perhaps if we went back to the speedway, and I took a better look at it, explained certain things to you . . . Then, if you still think that a fifteen-percent interest is equal to the sum that's missing, I won't quibble." Taking her silence for agreement, he released her and went back to his desk. He leaned down to press a buzzer on the intercom, and told the secretary who answered that he was leaving for the day.

"I was thinking," he told her as he led her to the elevator that took them to the underground garage, "that if we both went in my car, you could show me the speedway, then I could take you home, you could change into something frilly, and we could come back here to dinner. How does that strike you?"

I'd sooner dine with a rabid dog, she thought irately, but she managed to smile as she accepted, recalling just in time her need to charm this audacious man out of his desire to send her brother to prison.

The southbound traffic was heavy. Maile watched his hands as Jake maneuvered the sleek red Ferrari in and out of jams. They were strong hands, well-manicured yet masculine-hard. Disregarding the strange feelings this action invited, she raised her eyes to his face. He seemed to be wrestling with a difficult problem, if she could tell by the way he was frowning. His knuckles were turning white on the wheel. Maile glanced at the speedometer and shuddered. For a man who was vehemently against speedways and racing in general, he drove faster on the freeways than any racer she had ever known. She ached to tell this infuriatingly complex man that he was breaking the law but wisely kept her thoughts to herself.

"Frightened?" he murmured derisively, slanting her a doubting glance.

"Not in the least, Mr. Weston," she returned with some semblance of calm despite her racing heart. "I've been conditioned by experts who have driven at higher speeds, but only where there was no chance of hurting innocent people." Her cold rebuke seemed only to amuse him, and since she had meant to insult him, she settled back in her seat with an air of annoyance, and a furious determination to avoid further conversation with him.

The weather was typical for March in the Bay Area: cool, with the smell of rain in the air. Fluffy clouds edged in black moved overhead, giving her a clue to tomorrow's weather. Maile shivered, and wished she had thought to wear a coat.

As the speed of the Ferrari increased, so did her apprehensions. Dear God! Why had she ever agreed to ride with him? *I must've been crazy!* But no, she had had a perfectly good reason for behaving so impulsively; she had hoped to change his mind about *persecuting* Bryan. For that's what it was: he just could not bring himself to believe that perhaps his father, in his senility, had made a financial blunder. Bryan had gone out on a limb for Charles Weston, and now his son was right there, maliciously determined to chop the limb down, not caring that Bryan was innocent.

White, green, red, blue, yellow—these were the colors of the flags unfurled and waving in the early-evening breeze as the red sports car turned off the highway onto the narrow road leading down to the speedway.

A minute later Jake stopped his car outside the gate, and Maile went to open it. Jake leaned his elbow against the window, resting his chin on his fist, and revved his engine while Maile fumbled with the padlock. She knew he was purposely trying to make her nervous, but she'd be damned if she'd let him know that he was succeeding.

The car raced through the open gate, throwing a light blanket of dust over Maile. Sputtering, she called Jake a few choice names under her breath, then dusted herself off and followed him in.

In the semidarkness of the spring evening, the stands that ringed the track cast eerie shadows against the fence. Maile felt a stab of pain, nostalgically recalling some of the dark dawns and late evenings she had opened the same gate for Mike.

Jake eyed her curiously as she came abreast of him. "On a good day, how much do you bring in?" he asked abruptly, turning away from her.

Maile shrugged. Those were things Mike had never discussed with her, and she had never pried into his business. "That's something you'll have to take up with my accountant. He's the Farraday of Farraday and Douglass, his office is on Van Ness in the city."

He made a notation on a pad he had taken from his shirt pocket, then turned to cast an appraising glance over her.

"And you? Did you always come with the speedway?" The question was so unexpected, so insulting, that Maile stared up at him in a state of near shock. To make matters worse, she felt her face flush hotly, and was thankful for the darkness that hid her embarrassment from him.

"Not that it's any of your business, Mr. Weston, but I

was engaged to the former owner, Michael Sloan." Her voice was quiet, giving no hint of the turmoil in her breast.

"Was?" Reaching down, he captured her left hand in his. "Was?" he repeated, his voice silky soft, and now there was interest in the depths of his eyes as he rubbed his thumb lightly over the imprint left by Mike's ring.

Maile shivered with revulsion. This man's audacity went beyond belief! "He died," she said stiffly, giving a tug on her hand. His grip held.

"And left you this. *Very* nice." His tone and the unnecessary emphasis he placed on the adverb left little doubt in Maile's mind as to what he was implying. She drew a deep breath to control her fiery temper and pulled again on her hand. He would not release it. She swore mentally, and stood rigidly facing him while his eyes roamed with insolent ease over her flushed face, down the creamy soft column of her neck, and down to the rising and falling movement of her breasts. Maile shivered inwardly, involuntarily, feeling naked under that penetrating look.

"And now your brother has plunged another man's assets into indebtedness." His voice was deliberately rude.

Maile glared up at him with hot impotent anger. "You have no right to say that." Again she tugged on her hand, and this time he released it. Clasping her trembling fingers tightly in her other hand, she lifted her face to his, her eyes bright with disdain. "I suppose you judge everyone by your own behavior, and that's why you can't understand that it was my decision to help Bryan. We share everything, Mr. Weston, good or bad. But I don't suppose a cold fish like you would know anything about sharing. . . ." Wanting only to inflict a hurt, she added caustically, "It's no wonder your poor nephew ran away from you!"

There was a second of shocked silence during which the only sound he made was the sharp intake of his breath.

He cast a menacing shadow over her as he leaned toward her. Maile steeled herself to suffer his touch, expecting to be hurt, but when his fingers gripped her shoulders, they were unbelievably gentle. Very slowly she lifted her face to his, totally confused. The dig she had made must have certainly angered him, if not *hurt* him. She released her pent-up breath slowly.

"You're right, Maile Riordan," he said in a voice so quiet, so sweet, so warm, it washed over her like smooth, golden honey. "But I'm always willing to learn," he added in a whisper that was like a caress against her dry lips as he bent further, at the same time capturing the hand she had raised to ward him off. There was a brief second when Maile thought she could escape him, but then his lips were touching hers, and she was too stunned by the feelings fluttering inside her to do more than stand there, frozen, letting him take what he wanted from her mouth.

No! she screamed—but in her mind, as she felt her body flood with a treacherous warmth. Until now, only Mike had ever made her feel so trembly inside, so whole, so quiveringly vibrant. Maile turned and twisted desperately against him, hating the sensations his warm mouth moving against hers was making her feel. Knees that seemed to have turned to jelly buckled under her, but she was kept from falling by the muscular arm that went down to her waist and lifted her gently against his warm male body. Maile's senses reeled as his kiss deepened and his hands began a bold exploration of the body pressed to his. Annoyed because she was disturbingly aware of his body's reaction to her nearness, Maile tried again to release herself. But his arm tightened around her waist, holding her to him.

Dear God, would he never be done with her? Panic gripped her, and at the touch of his tongue probing, lightly caressing the moist, inner flesh of her mouth, she made one last desperate attempt to break free.

For a few moments after he had removed his mouth from hers, she leaned against him, feeling the strength and hardness of his chest beneath her cheek. As she regained her equilibrium, her mind began to function away from the feel of his breath on her cheek, the warmth of his mouth as it merged with hers. She stepped away, willing strength into legs that still felt rubbery.

"That was all right for a beginning," he mocked as he reached out to keep her from leaving him. Then, one finger tilting her face to his, he added, "You're a warm-blooded, vibrant woman after all, Maile Riordan, despite the hardened career woman facade with which you tried to deceive me."

His words served to strengthen her resolve not to let him see just how much his kiss had affected her. Maile lifted her chin fractionally, escaped his hand, and stepped away.

"Tell me," she said as she took another step away from him, "was *this* your intention in coming here, or were you seriously considering my proposition?" she finished doubtfully, giving him her back.

"I was considering a great number of things, Maile," he murmured, coming to stand behind her, close but not touching, "among them the very appealing notion of becoming your . . . partner." The slight pause before that final word, together with the kiss he pressed against her neck, made Maile draw in her breath in an audible gasp.

She had sufficient reason to fly into a rage, but she managed to control her temper. "I see."

Cursing herself for being a fool, for believing he had come to the speedway to evaluate it, she walked stiffly away from him and stood, a slight, dark figure against the blackness slowly descending upon them.

Gradually her anger subsided, and she became aware of the night and the sounds around her; the rustling in the tall grass outside the fence, the chirping of crickets. A dog barked somewhere, and an owl hooted far away as the moon slid from behind a cluster of black clouds and cast its pale glow upon the scene. For a long time she stood without moving, and stared unseeing at the empty bleachers, her mind whirling with thought. What had possessed her to go to this man and offer him Mike's speedway as collateral? Likely as not, he would eventually find the missing money and never admit it to her.

He might even find a way to close down the speedway legally because of that nephew of his. A sense of failure washed over her; she had abused Mike's trust. She had tried to be the sort of woman he had believed she could be, and yet, the first time she had found herself in difficulties, she had placed his precious speedway in the hands of a mercenary. The sense of failure soured her mouth and iced her heart.

Turning swiftly with bitter resolution, Maile walked back to Jake. He was leaning negligently against his car, arms folded across his muscular chest, looking omnipotent and smugly satisfied. In a cold, unfriendly voice she told him she wanted to go back to San Francisco and her car.

"And our dinner?" he murmured.

Maile shrugged. She didn't care if she never ate again,

particularly not with him. "You're getting your pound of flesh with your share of Mike's speedway. What more do you want from me?" She stifled the sigh that started to rise to her throat at the gleam of desire she noted in his eyes as they roamed over her.

She hurried around the car, and when he was about to reach out to open the door for her, she opened it and slid onto her seat, closing the door before he could. When he was sitting behind the wheel, he reached into his coat pocket and brought out his cigarettes. Silently he lighted two, and offered her one. Maile curtly refused it.

"No bad habits?" His expression seemed to taunt, but he stubbed the second cigarette in the car ashtray without wording his thoughts.

He set the key in the ignition but did not start the car. "I'm hungry, and I don't see any valid reason why two silent partners can't have dinner together, do you?" He took a drag on his cigarette and blew the smoke out of the corner of his mouth, his eyes intent on her.

"I'm not hungry," she said stiffly, releasing her pent-up breath in an impotently angry sigh. She had to escape him. She had to outrun the warm womanly feelings this wicked man purposely—and so easily—aroused in her.

"I am." He turned the key in the ignition and drove out of the grounds. He stopped, got out of the car, and went back to lock the gate before Maile could open her door to do it herself.

"Light me a cigarette, won't you?" he asked as he slid behind the wheel of his sleek red Ferrari.

Grudgingly Maile did as he asked, and handed him the cigarette with a hand that seemed to tremble more as it came closer to his. And the awful man knew it, too, damn him! she thought.

"Thanks," he breathed, putting the car into gear and accelerating gently so as not to jostle her. Maile, who had been expecting him to move out so swiftly, it would make her head snap back, turned curious eyes to his face and found him smiling.

He did not consult her, but drove into San Jose, where he stopped at the first restaurant that took his fancy. Ill-humoredly Maile left the car when he opened her door and followed him into the restaurant, telling herself she was not going to eat.

But, to her undying chagrin, she discovered that she was hungry, and though she would have liked to throw what he ordered for her in his arrogant face, she ate slowly, savoring every bite of her coquilles St. Jacques.

His hunger sated, Jake leaned back against the padded backrest and lighted a cigarette. Through the smoke that curled upward, veiling his expression, he watched her, the expression in his blue eyes further hidden by the fringe of dark lashes that drooped slightly.

"Were your father and brother into racing too? Or are you the only one interested in racers?"

Ignoring his double meaning, Maile returned in a slightly nostalgic voice, "Our father was small-time, but he had a dream of someday racing at the Indy Five Hundred. Unfortunately he and our mother died before he'd had a chance to really work up to it.

"He had an engine he'd hoped to market someday." She smiled. "Mom called him a cockeyed optimist, a fanciful dreamer, but I know he would've achieved his dream if he'd lived."

"And your brother?" he asked sharply.

"Bryan? Bryan was always interested in helping Dad in his computations, but he never really liked cars. In fact,

48

he's very much like you. He hates racing and everyone associated with the sport."

A shadow descended over his handsome features. "And you? Would you race if you had the proper vehicle?"

"Very probably." Thinking of Mike's reasons for driving at dizzying speeds, she added coyly, "There's a crazy kind of freedom I feel when I'm out there on the track—a delicious, tingling thrill from head to toe."

"Surely you could get the same thrill out of something else? An intimate relationship with a man, maybe."

"I doubt it," she snapped, pushing her coffee cup away. She wished again that she had never agreed to ride with him. How much simpler things would have been if she had her own car. She would simply get up, go to it, and leave this audacious and arrogant man sitting here by himself.

"I don't suppose you'd care to put it to a test?" he challenged softly.

Not with you, I wouldn't, she thought, cursing herself for the slight tremor that shook her body with his bold eyes so intent on her lips.

"I didn't think so," he mocked silkily. Smiling at some private joke, he stood up, at the same time reaching into his pocket for his wallet.

Weakly the moon filtered its silvery beams through the layer of rain clouds gathering overhead, as if determined to throw some light over the two silent figures walking to the low-slung car parked across the street from the restaurant.

"Not this time," Jake muttered as Maile started to open her own door. He saw that she was settled comfortably, and gently closed the door.

The smooth movements of the sports car over a near-deserted freeway, plus her own desire to withdraw from her newly acquired partner, lulled Maile into a restless sleep. Curling herself into a tight little ball against the door, she gave in to the languorous feeling that washed over her, and closed her eyes.

Maile woke with a sense of panic clutching at her breast, and for a moment she could not remember who this man was who was gently shaking her, urging her in a silky voice to wake up.

"Where are we?" she mumbled, glancing around her at the unfamiliar territory: the towering bulk of a house outlined in the dark to her right, the well-groomed hedges lining the sloping drive. And the silence that surrounded them.

"Home . . . my home," he told her amusedly as Maile rapidly blinked the sleep from her eyes. "It's much too late for you to be driving home, and besides, you're too sleepy."

Maile's head jerked back to look at the house, then turned to look at Jake, only to find him again smiling in that nerve-racking way of his.

"No, thanks," she retorted. "I want to go home."

"Stop being so childish," he said sternly. "I've no ulterior motive in asking you to stay, if that's what you're worried about. My nephew lives with me. If he doesn't make you feel safe, there's a bedroom with a heavy lock on the door that would keep even a more determined man than me out of your bed." He slanted her an indulgent glance, and smiled briefly. "Trust me."

"I want to go back to my car," she said stiffly, about as eager to trust him as she would be to trust a rattlesnake.

"What's the matter?" he mocked with an edge of frustrated anger in his tone. "Afraid to trust me? Or are you afraid to trust yourself with me?" But even as he was taunting her, he was turning the key in the ignition.

With a sigh of relief Maile settled back down on the bucket seat and lightly rested her head against the window.

Maile was never so thankful as she was when Jake stopped his car behind hers. She thanked him politely as she left his car and agreed to meet with him the following day to conclude their business. She stumbled a little as she went in front of his headlights. To her surprise and dismay Jake was immediately beside her, holding her up. She had not even heard his door open! Swiftly she jerked away, for the nearness of him disturbed her equilibrium. *It's just that I'm tired*, she thought, excusing herself, but she knew— deep down in her secret self she knew—that it was something else. She was lonely, hungry for the feel of a man's arms around her. She felt guilty, ashamed of her feelings and strangely disloyal to Mike's memory.

"Are you all right?" His voice washed over her warmly, and she shivered. His hands moved down to her hips, slowly bringing her closer to him.

"I'm fine," she returned frigidly, moving out of his arms. She turned from him and started to insert her key into the lock, but his hand closed over hers, stopping her.

"Don't go, Maile." It was said in a low, intimate tone that sent a shiver racing up her spine and made her pulses jump. She felt herself caught and turned quickly to find him regarding her with a dark, passionate gleam in his eyes.

"I didn't know a woman could look so damned sexy all tousled and sleepy," he murmured, bending toward her.

"No!" But even as the word erupted from her mouth, Maile was moving up to meet his lips.

"No?" He laughed huskily. "You're tired, lady, or else your mind and your body are not in accord." Arms that were tantalizingly gentle brought her against the hardness of the tall male body, and his mouth came down over hers in a kiss that was more devastating in its tenderness than any violence he could have inflicted upon her. With something like a sob Maile went limp in his arms, helplessly answering his kiss. There was no thought of resistance in her mind, yet it seemed he was afraid she would leave him, and tightened his arms almost painfully around her slender form. His kiss deepened. Despite herself, Maile felt an uprush of desire in response to his experienced and demanding mouth.

When he finally put her away from him, Maile was gasping for breath. "Wh—why did you do that?" Her voice was hoarse with panic.

He smiled, and his eyes touched her, moved over her predatorily, marking possession of the mouth his mouth had ravished, the curves his large hands had explored. "It felt like the right thing to do," he murmured, smiling.

"Well, it wasn't!"

"For my part, it was," he contradicted suavely. Taking the key from her hand, he opened her door and urged her into the car.

"I'll talk to your accountant in the morning, early, and then I'll have my lawyer draw up a contract for you to sign. It'll be ready by the time you get here." He smiled crookedly. "Come early and I'll let you buy me lunch," he added, then closed the door gently after making sure that she had the key in the ignition. He rapped his hard knuckles on the roof of her car, turned, and went back to his own car.

Maile shivered. What was happening to her? She shook

her head, trying to clear it of the confusion he had injected into her. Mechanically she started the car and moved it slowly out of the parking space. She gave a shaky sigh. What could she do? Whom could she turn to for advice? She gripped the wheel until her knuckles drained of color. She was trapped. She could do nothing but continue with her disorganized plan to pay the Weston Corporation what Bryan had lost.

Bryan! But no, she could not talk to him about what that audacious man had done. Never! Whatever the cost—and it looked as if it would be steep—he must be kept from knowing what he had innocently plunged her into. Somehow or other, she had to brazen this thing out, deal with that dark, disturbing man by herself.

CHAPTER 3

Maile felt doomed. Not only was she shaken by thoughts of Jake Weston's disturbing behavior all the way home, she made the mistake of calling her brother as soon as she had taken a cool, reviving bath.

"Maile, do you know what time it is?" Bryan's drowsiness did not hide the annoyance in his tone. "Good Lord, girl, it's not even six!"

"Well, *excuse* me!" She reached up a hand to rub the suddenly throbbing area above the bridge of her nose, at the same time wiping away the tear that had slipped out of the corner of one eye. "I thought you *might* be interested in knowing that Weston went for the deal I made him."

"Maile. . . ." Bryan's voice came out in an indrawn breath. "That's good, honey. Oh, I knew you could do it."

Liar! "I'm going back to the city to sign the contract he's having drawn up this morning."

"Did he—did he say anything about me, Maile?" His tone was pathetically hopeful. "I mean, about my job?"

"Did you need to ask that, Bryan?" Maile felt vaguely irritated. Suddenly she felt older than he, more mature, and impatient with his dependency on her, his junior by ten years. When had this switch in responsibilities come about? she wondered, seeing their role reversals for the first time. It frightened her, and that fear put an edge to her normally soft voice. "It wasn't my place to ask him about your job, Bryan. Why don't you talk to him, find out what your position is, now that he's been assured that the missing money is going to be paid back?"

A sigh came over the wire, and then, "All right, honey," he said in a tone dripping with weariness. "And thanks. Someday I'll make it all up to you, honey."

I know you will, she thought, but she didn't get the chance to say the words to him. She heard the click at his end of the line, and set her phone down gently. Her hand still touching the phone, she scanned the room with a sudden urgent need to be reassured that nothing had changed. And nothing had—not in this room, this house. Mike's furniture, his trophies, his posters and pictures were all around her. The macrame hanger she had made while Mike was in Indianapolis two years ago was still in the corner of the room where the light from the window struck it, putting a vibrancy to the fading gold threads braided into the cords.

Sighing with weariness, she went into her bedroom. She removed her robe, letting it fall slowly to the floor. Her eyes wandered over to her water bed, and she sighed with longing. She was bone-weary, and wished she could just forget about going to see Weston, crawl in under her furry bedspread and sheets, and allow the warmth of the water bed to soothe away her tiredness. But she knew she couldn't. Maybe she would be dead on her feet by early afternoon; maybe she would be too tired to return home; maybe she would end up having to spend the night in the city—the maybes were innumerable. One fact remained unchanged: She had to meet with Jake Weston, no matter how tired she was, no matter how much she dreaded another meeting with him.

Her hands shook as she pulled on a pair of white bell bottom jeans and a blue silk blouse. The zipper caught, and she swore. Freeing it, she zipped it fully, then tucked in the blouse around her narrow waist.

Why am I so nervous? She took a deep, quieting breath and smiled as she realized that she did not have to be with Jake longer than it took to sign a contract. *I'll sign the damned thing, then split.* There was no shame in retreat—particularly when she knew the effect that wretched man had on her.

That thought brought a measure of relief, and she was able to smile as she sat down to do her hair. Thank God for chignons, she thought, twirling her heavy hair into one and securing the bun with a handful of pins. She was not trying to impress the man, so she settled for just a dab of eyeshadow and a light coat of lipstick.

Maile thought it portentous when she found the same parking place that she had had the day before and hoped fervently that it was an indication that everything would go smoothly for her.

As she walked to the Weston Building she stiffened her spine with resolution. She would not sign anything until *he* agreed not to interfere in the operation of the speedway. But as her steps brought her closer to her adversary, she realized that she would sign *anything,* agree to almost anything, to bring her meeting with Jake Weston to a speedy conclusion.

"Go right in, he's expecting you," the receptionist, who seemed to have been watching the door for her, said coyly as she ran a speculative eye over Maile's trim figure.

"Thank you." Her steps evenly paced and firm, she walked down the long corridor and knocked on Jake's door.

"You're prompt; that's good," Jake approved with a smile as he opened the door to her. "I like that in a woman." His eyes ran appreciatively over her; his smile widened, showing almost all his teeth.

Maile was in no frame of mind to return his smile. She looked him up and down, the designer in her approving the change she found in the tall lean frame. Under a tan coat he was wearing a brown turtleneck knit shirt that was tucked into the slim waist of his dark-brown slacks.

His desk, too, had undergone a change. Gone were the piles of papers, the books, the folders, the paperweights that had cluttered it on her last visit. The entire office was neater; the small chair in which he had invited her to sit was closer to the desk, set at an angle to his massive leather chair. On the desktop were four copies of the contract she had come to sign.

Sign them and get out of here, urged the cautious little voice inside Maile Riordan, and she moved forward to obey it. Her hand trembling slightly, she lifted a pen from his desk and signed the first copy.

"Wait!" Jake was suddenly beside her, his hand on her wrist. "We need a witness to make it all proper," he said, flashing her a smile while his fingers gently pried the pen loose from her hand. "I'll be right back," he added, throwing the pen down on the desk. "Why don't you make yourself comfortable? Take my chair."

You would have to be handsome, Maile thought sourly

as she watched him walk away. Why couldn't you have been in your sixties, with a limp, a bulbous nose, overlarge ears, bulging eyes! But he wasn't. Even his teeth were perfect, and he flashed them at every opportunity. A man with his smile simply could not be trusted. A handsome, mocking man with *his* track record a century earlier would have been rightfully called a rake, and mamas with pride and sensibility would have hidden their young daughters where he couldn't find them.

Taking advantage of her few moments alone, Maile went back to the contracts, and hurriedly read through the one she had already signed. *Thirty percent* jumped out at her, and she blinked with confusion. Thirty percent! when she had reconciled herself to letting him have the forty percent just to make their partnership as brief as possible. She shook her head in defeat. There was just no understanding that man.

Jake came in, his receptionist a step behind him.

"Now you may sign," he said amiably, handing her the pen. As she took it his eyes went over her, almost possessively, and for one brief crazy minute the image of a wolf licking his chops flashed through Maile's mind. She shuddered, banishing that image, and quickly signed the three remaining copies of their contract.

The deed was done. Maile experienced a sense of foreboding as Jake dismissed his receptionist, thanking her curtly for her help. As the door closed behind the girl he turned to take two copies of the contract from his desk.

"One for your files, and one for your lawyer's files," he said as he held them out to her.

"And now that that's over, where would you like to go for lunch?"

With you, no place. But she cleared her throat, and

forced calmness into her voice. "I'm sorry, Mr. Weston. I can't stay. But before I go, I believe there are a few ground rules we must establish concerning the track."

Eyes that sparkled like sapphires roamed her face slowly, searching her forced-bland expression, narrowing as they lingered on the stubborn set to her jaw. A steely look crept into them. "And the first one will be that I keep my big nose out of your seventy percent of the business, which I take to mean that I should stay completely the hell away from both the track and you."

"It isn't as if you liked the speedway . . . As for me, Mr. Weston, I am very particular who my friends are." *There, that's putting you in your place, you puffed up, arrogant man!*

Glittering blue eyes boldly roamed over her slender form, taking their time as they journeyed from her slim waist to her narrow hips, then down the length of her legs and up again to her face. "I wasn't asking to be your friend," he drawled insultingly. "I had a more intimate relationship in mind."

Maile's hackles rose along with the color that tinted her cheeks. The nerve of the man! After blackmailing her into handing over to him nearly a third of her business, he had the colossal audacity to flirt with her! She tried to stare him down, only to have her own gaze falter and fall. She did a slow burn, and felt a strange sensation in the pit of her stomach which she attributed to frustration because she felt completely out of her depths with this miserable man.

It was the height of arrogance to think that she would lower herself to having an affair with him. "That is not possible," she managed to say, forcing herself to meet his steady blue gaze.

His lips twitched. "Everything is possible, Maile, if you know how to go after what you want," he murmured. Stepping closer to her, he reached out and took a stray tendril of black hair between his thumb and forefinger.

"I've always prided myself in speaking bluntly. . . . I want you, Maile Riordan, and I intend to have you." As he spoke he twisted the lock of hair around his finger, forcing her to step closer to him.

Struck speechless by his outrageousness, Maile could only stare up at him as he lifted her hair to his lips. In spite of herself, she began to tremble.

"Ah, Maile," he breathed, "you cannot imagine how lovely, how very desirable you are, standing here looking like you'd like to do me in." Chuckling, he released her hair and went back to sit on the edge of his desk, swinging one foot free of the floor. He looked at her for long moments before he spoke again.

"You can relax, Miss Riordan," he said, his tone sober, his expression bland. "Today we will behave like business partners, and nothing more. Now . . . I will agree to stay away from the track, provided you agree to a condition of mine."

Maile had not had the strength to reply before, nor to protest his bold caress, but now that she suspected he was about to interfere in the management of the speedway, she managed to find her voice. "What is it you want this time?" she demanded tartly.

"Whenever you have these 'grudge races' of yours where, as I understand it, the driver needs only a valid California driver's license to compete, you will see to it that my nephew is not allowed to enter into the competition."

Maile's breath was drawn in on an audible gasp. Who

the devil did he think he was, ordering her around? "Thirty percent of the business does not give you the right to tell me who to let in and who not to," she stated, forcing calm into her voice when, instead, she felt like screaming the words at him.

"If you don't want your nephew competing, then *you* keep him away from the speedway. As long as the boys pay their entry fees, I have no intention of turning a single one of them away, *no matter how closely related he is to you!*"

His eyes spoke of burning anger as he stood up and came back to where she stood, inwardly trembling but defiantly meeting his gaze. He towered above her, his glacial expression demanding that she knuckle down and agree to his condition. Maile refused to cower. With forced bravado she folded her arms across her breast and tilted her head back to stare him in the face. She knew he would retaliate, and expected him to go so far as to try to renege on their deal just to get his own way, but she refused to back down.

"Perhaps you're right," he capitulated, much to her surprise. "Arthur's my problem, not yours."

Arthur. Maile smiled and breathed a sigh of relief. "We really have no problem, Mr. Weston," she started, with a silent prayer in her heart thanking the good Lord that she did not know this man's nephew. "You see, I do not know any Arthur, so—"

"I know he'll show up, Maile," he interrupted, his tone confident. He hesitated for a moment, certain she would bolt like a skittish colt if he came on too strong. "But like I said before, he's my problem."

Maile acknowledged this admission with a wary smile. He had given in too easily. What could he be planning now? Could she trust him? Was he, even now, thinking of a way to prevent her opening the speedway? She eyed the door with a longing to pass through it and never see this man again. Perhaps she ought to go from here to see Jim Boyden and find out, in layman's terms this time, exactly how much power she had innocently placed in Jake Weston's hands. She looked down at the contract in her hands, wishing she'd read it thoroughly, carefully, before signing it, and wondering, too, if it would be too late to back out of it if Jim told her she had made a rotten bargain.

He was speaking, but Maile was still battling with her own thoughts. She glanced up at him with a start when she felt his hand on her cheek.

"I—I'm sorry, I didn't hear what you were saying," she apologized, stepping away from that marauding hand.

"Is that so?" The lean bronzed face was amused. "Day-dreaming, eh?" he teased. His smile was so charming, she hated him for it. She felt her pulses quickening and knew that she had to get away from him.

"I must be going. I have to fit a friend's daughter for a party dress," she said, turning and reaching across the chair for her purse.

"No, you don't."

"How would you know that?" She drew a deep breath for control and turned to face him.

"The truth is, you're afraid to have lunch with me, Maile. Admit it."

"Afraid?" Cynical disbelief widened the eyes she lifted to his face, and her mouth curved with a smile that was little more than a derisive grin. "Did it ever occur to you, Mr. Weston, that I might not *want* to have anything to do with you?" Carefully she adjusted the strap of her purse across her shoulder and prepared to leave.

"Is that right?" he countered in a drawling voice that raised the hair on her arms. The hard mouth curled rather cynically as he closed the distance between them. And as he bent over her, Maile became uncomfortably aware of the good clean male odor of him—and she cringed with shame at the sensual thoughts that immediately raced through her mind.

"Come on, let's have lunch," he whispered, his tone silky and disturbing to her already agitated nerves. "I promise to behave myself, no matter how provocative you are."

Panicking, Maile started edging her way toward the door. "No, thank you, Mr. Weston. I do have an appointment."

"It was canceled. I talked to your partner a few minutes after she'd opened the shop, and told her you were going to be with me all day." He laughed low in his throat, arching one mocking brow at her as she doubled her hands into fists at her sides.

Maile could not find the words with which to consign him and his high-handed manner to damnation. And then, her voice hoarse with anger, she sputtered, "Just where do you come off interfering in my life like that? You have a lot of nerve, Mr. Weston!" She moved to the door, but he stopped her with a low-voiced challenge.

"Prove you're not afraid of being with me, Maile."

Her Irish pride rose swiftly to the surface, and she turned around to face him, a very cold smile parting her lips as she started to take up his challenge. But a cautioning little voice within told her it would be a mistake to accept, and so she replied, "I don't have to prove anything to anyone, Mr. Weston, but particularly not to someone like you." And again she turned to go.

"Not so fast, Maile." His voice came from much too close, making Maile jump. In the next instant his hands were on her shoulders, spinning her around. Senses reeling with surprise, Maile stared up at his face in disbelief, angry words tumbling in her mind, yet not quite reaching her lips.

"Can't you get it through that pretty head of yours that I'm not going to take no for an answer from you?"

Swift anger overrode her shock, and Maile spat out, "And can't you get it through your thick skull that I have no intention of spending my precious time with you?" Her eyes in meeting his could display only derision.

Blue eyes glittering with anger stared into hers. He did not like being thwarted; and this girl and her crook of a brother *owed* him—and he meant to collect. For a moment another face was superimposed on hers, and he winced with the memory of another woman who had come on to him with a sweetly innocent facade that hid the heart of a mercenary little bitch.

"You have no choice but to indulge my whims, Maile," he told her, his voice grating. "You want me to stay away from the speedway, remember? And, too, you wouldn't want me to put out the word that Bryan Riordan is a bad employment risk, now, would you?" he challenged, his voice now deceptively mellow.

His whims. Maile shivered with apprehension. And looking into his eyes, she knew why she felt that way. The raw hunger she saw in his eyes made her realize with a flash of insight why he had agreed to a seventy-thirty split rather than insisting on the forty percent he had originally wanted. Silently she cursed herself for falling so neatly into his trap; she should have known this man was the type who gave up an inch only to take a foot. His bold, triumphant look gave her a clue to his thoughts, and she knew without a doubt that he expected to have *her* in place of the extra ten percent. Anger directed at Bryan for the mess he had embroiled her in smote her, and she trembled convulsively under Jake's harsh grip on her shoulders.

"You can let me go now, Mr. Weston," she whispered. "I'm not going anywhere."

He released her almost reluctantly. "You have no choice but to indulge my whims. . . ." His words echoed harshly in her mind again and again as she watched him cross the room to his desk. His whims. . . . Maile's breath caught in her throat as her eyes surveyed the virile frame stretching across the desk as Jake was reaching for the intercom.

Jake spoke to one of his secretaries for a moment, then he came back to where Maile stood waiting for him by the door.

Maile let him take her by the arm as they went out into the corridor. Then, as he turned to close his office door, she pried herself loose. He smiled at her move, and the glance he gave her told her with bold certainty that he could take much more than her arm if he set his mind to it. Her eyebrow went up challengingly, but she said nothing.

"I found this nice little place," he told her as they went out into the suddenly hazy day. "It's not far—and it's worth the walk."

Clouds pregnant with rain had gathered overhead, throwing the city into semidarkness. The breeze coming in from the Bay gently caressed Maile's face, cooling the anger that had flushed her cheeks. She drew her coat closer about her and reluctantly started walking beside Jake.

"Here we are," he announced a few minutes later, stopping at what Maile at first believed to be an alleyway. "They make your sandwiches and salads to order. It's inexpensive too," he threw in with some irony. "I thought you'd like to know, in case you're one of those females who believe in paying her own way."

"Why should I?" Maile retorted, unwittingly confirming his suspicions that she was like all the others, out to get whatever she could from a man. "It wasn't my idea to come to lunch." Angrily she tossed back the few wisps of black hair that had fallen across her face and preceded Jake into the restaurant.

Towering above everyone else in the room, Jake easily spotted a table in the corner. He led her promptly to it, settled her down, and left to make a phone call.

Maile was relieved to see him go, taking advantage of his absence to glance over her surroundings. She found she liked the restaurant. It had atmosphere, and was apparently very popular with nine-to-fivers, for it was crowded to capacity.

If only she were here with someone she truly liked, she told herself with a sigh. Maile frowned darkly, wondering what grievous sin she had committed—and against whom —to deserve someone like Jake Weston as a punishment.

"Frowning causes wrinkles," Jake teased as he eased himself onto the seat next to her. "Or are you just near-sighted, and too vain to wear glasses?"

Maile shrugged.

This was no good. Jake looked down at the unhappy face turned from him and flinched. This was not what he had had in mind.

"I know I asked you to lunch, Maile," he began in an apologetic tone, "but I'm going to have to give you a rain

66

check. Something came up at the office, and I have to go back. I hope you understand. . . ." He stood up, offering her his hand.

"Will you come back and have lunch with me on Friday?"

"Do I have any choice?" she challenged hatefully.

The expression that flitted briefly across his ruggedly handsome face told her that her answer had not only surprised him, it had hurt him as well. *Impossible!* rang through Maile's doubting mind. Men like Jake Weston had skin as thick and hard as a turtle's shell; a woman's rejection seldom went deeper than the epidermis.

"No. No, you don't," he said, his tone quiet, and cold.

I didn't think so, Maile thought miserably, shiveringly aware of his proximity and his warmth, as well as the quickening of her pulses as his fingers closed around her arm. Her eyes skimmed upward to his expression, and she had no doubt that he knew how he rattled her senses and worse, that he took great pride in it!

A drizzling rain was falling when Jake escorted her out of the restaurant. The air was fresh and clean; the sidewalks slightly damp and slippery. She would be soaked by the time she reached her car, Maile thought as she looked down at her open-toed shoes, but there was nothing she could do about it. Drawing her coat closer about her shivering form, she bowed her head and started away.

"Wait." Jake reached out and pulled her back. "You're not exactly dressed for a stroll in the rain," he mocked in a tone as soft and sweet as one a man might use on his lover. Very gently he drew her flush against him, and she shivered. "I'll get us a taxi," he murmured, his mouth so close to her ear, his breath was a soft caress on her neck.

Maile shivered again, but it was not because of the rain

falling softly on her toes. "I don't mind walking," she told him stiffly, licking the rain off her lips, thankful it was cool against her feverish skin. She started away again, but he tightened his hold on her arm, drawing her back to him.

"Don't be silly. You'll get drenched." He hauled her roughly against him and held her so tightly, she could feel his heart beating against her arm.

"I don't mind, really," she insisted, tugging at her arm.

"But I do," he murmured. "I don't want you to get cold, especially at a time when I can do nothing to get you warm again." The sound of his laughter grated in her ears and increased Maile's desire to put a safe distance between them.

"You stay here; I'll go call a cab." Giving her arm a gentle squeeze, Jake released her and went quickly back into the restaurant.

Maile threw a quick glance over her shoulder, saw that he was already inside the restaurant, and took off on a run.

About fifteen minutes later she was in her car, shivering with cold from head to toe, and breathless from running. Her hand trembled as she inserted the key in the ignition. She started the car and sat there for a few minutes while it warmed. Once the warmth began to spread through her frozen limbs and she could feel her toes, she set the car in gear and slid carefully into traffic. Her hair had come undone in the running, and she tossed it from her face with a sigh. She took a deep breath to quiet her erratically beating heart and concentrated her attention on her driving.

"What a coward you are!" She could almost hear Mike taunting her. Without conscious intent her mind conjured up his dear face, the amused vision of him she remembered best—his rugged features creased with silent laughter.

And she remembered with a wistful smile that she had tried to run from him, too, but he had pursued her with gentle determination and had finally convinced her she had nowhere to run but to him.

Had Mike ever filled her with this wild warring of emotions that set her teeth on edge, as Jake somehow managed to do? No, never. Mike had subtly coaxed her into his arms; Jake had grabbed her with supreme arrogance. What Mike had taken with persuasive charm, Jake would take with arrogant assurance. Where Mike had been impetuous and charming, Jake was perversely haughty and overbearing. She sighed dispiritedly. Was it possible for one woman to feel so strongly about two men who were worlds apart in everything that mattered to her?

What am I thinking?

The knowledge that, despite everything that had just happened, she was more than a little attracted to Jake Weston shook her and filled her with an unshakable sense of self-loathing. With a jerky movement she switched off the windshield wipers, then rolled down the car window and took a deep breath of damp, head-clearing air.

"Ah, Mike," she breathed ruefully, sighing for what was past and irrevocably lost. Nothing in her relationship with him or with her father and brother had prepared her to deal with a man of Jake Weston's stamp.

Lord, Bryan warned me that Jake was a chaser; why didn't I take heed and avoid the man like the plague? Why? She knew why, she thought sadly. For Bryan—because he was all she had left in the world. . . .

"Indulge his whims!" she spat out viciously, and with those words she felt her spine stiffening with resolution. She'd be damned if she'd become his puppet, she vowed, her mouth a tight line of determination. She would fight that man all the way, and if he wanted to fight dirty, then she'd fight him that way too. She smiled vindictively. If he tried to ruin Bryan, then she would search out his precious nephew, and—though the poor kid had done her no harm —she would use him to even up the score with Jake. And she would start by giving the boy a personal invitation to come use the track!

CHAPTER 4

Maile's confrontation with Jake had left her with an excess of nervous energy that even the long drive would not exhaust. She had to do something that would occupy both her hands and her mind. Driving faster than she normally did, she arrived at her boutique a few minutes before four.

"If Jake Weston calls, put him off. . . . Tell him you don't know where I am, or when I'll be back," Maile informed Ginny, her salesgirl–gal Friday as she breezed through the showroom on her way to the workroom. She repeated her message to Janey in a breathless tone, full of determination.

Janey glanced up from the pattern she had on the work-table and grinned. "Too late. He already called, about an hour ago. He said to tell you, and I quote: 'I'm not through with her, not by a long shot!' Said he would see you at eight at your house." Wrinkling her small nose, she gave a shake of her dark head. "When you pick 'em, boss, you really pick 'em!"

Maile was not amused, and her expression was enough to warn Janey away from the subject of Jake Weston. Damn! The man just wouldn't allow himself to be ignored! Maile hung her purse on a hook, then mentally rolled up her sleeves and went to work, determined to put Jake Weston and his autocratic manner completely out of her mind.

"Want to talk about it?" Janey asked curiously, after Maile had crumpled up and tossed into the wastebasket a sixth unsatisfactory design.

"Nothing to talk about," Maile replied distractedly, somewhat shortly. What did Jake want from her now? An apology for having run out on him? There was a stubborn streak a mile wide in Maile, and for a moment she toyed with the idea of not being at home for him. She tore off the last sheet in her sketchpad, crumpled it, and tossed it over her shoulder.

Damn him! Even when he was not physically present, he still managed to rattle her cage. A lump rose in her throat that would not dissolve no matter how many times she swallowed. She sniffed. To have gone from loving a tender, fun-loving, and compassionate man to feeling so positively wretched about a man who was the epitome of everything she despised!

Maile stared down at the fabric on the worktable, numb and miserable. She only half heard Janey talking excitedly, describing a costume she wanted to make using the smoky chiffon a smooth-talking salesman had dumped on them.

"We could put black spangles around the Mandarin collar," she said, and sighed with exasperation. "You're not listening."

No, she was not. Her mind was on Jake Weston . . . on the way his eyes crinkled when he smiled . . . on the way his lips twitched when he was amused . . . on the way he fit his clothes, and the way sensuality oozed from the man when he walked. She shuddered. It would be laughable, if only she did not hurt so much! A man she did not even like! How in the world could it be that he affected her in such a mind-bending way?

"Who shall we make the outfit for?" she asked, forcing her thoughts away from the dark, disturbing man who had left such an unsettling impression on her. She glanced at the shimmering fabric—a silvery turquoise lamé—Janey was bunching up in front of her.

"Verna Johnson, natch! She is the only tall *and thin* woman we know." Janey's voice was sharp and spiteful, quite unlike her usual sweet tone. Maile glanced up in surprise, then dismissed Janey's ill humor with a shrug. Perhaps the girl was upset because she would not confide in her.

"What do you suggest we do with it?"

"I told you, but you weren't listening to me!" Janey sighed, and shook her dark, curly head in exasperation. "All right, here goes again, but pay attention this time.

"The turquoise can be made into a long Mandarin-style gown with a slit on either side, hem-to-knee. Then the chiffon . . . an overdress with beaded cuffs and collar."

"The turquoise would look better as a lounging ensemble, with the chiffon in a long overblouse."

Janey shook her head. "No. My idea's better. Why don't you sketch both things, and then you'll see that I'm right." Her tone was tinged with annoyance.

Maile left the workroom and went into a small room at the back of the boutique that she used for her office. She spent the rest of the afternoon toying with designs with Mrs. Johnson in mind. Verna Johnson was tall, and she

73

had the thinness of a model. Married to an architect, with no children . . . pampered . . . and always able to afford whatever she wanted.

From the front of the shop she heard Ginny call out that she was leaving. Janey followed in her wake. Maile rubbed a hand across her tired eyes and put away her sketches. She might as well go home too. She needed a few minutes to herself before Jake came—a few minutes in which to bathe, and to think about how to receive him. Sighing, she slung her purse across her shoulder and left the shop.

Having Jake Weston as a partner in the speedway was proving extremely distasteful, she thought as she went out to her car.

When she answered the door at eight, she found Jake leaning indolently against the wall of the porch, smoking a cigarette.

"It's too pretty a night to be indoors, Maile," he drawled, flashing her his practiced smile. "Why don't we take a walk?"

Maile breathed a sigh of relief, and felt her shoulders relax. Until this moment she had not realized that her biggest fear was being alone with Jake inside her own house.

"That would be nice," she said, stepping out on the porch and letting the door slam behind her. Too late she recalled that the lock was temperamental—it locked when anyone slammed the door. Now she would have to use the extra key—and *he* would find out where she kept it. She didn't know why, but she sensed he would not hesitate to make use of that extra key. . . .

The rain had freshened the air. The night was comfortably cool, the air sweetly exhilarating. Above them the stars twinkled almost mischievously against a turquoise background; a pale moon sent its silvery fingers to play over the Pittosporum that lined her walk, setting the variegated leaves alight.

The moon seemed also to favor Jake, highlighting the planes of his face, putting a strange gleam in his eyes. Gone was the hard determination that she had sensed on their previous encounters. He was totally relaxed; he looked younger, despite the tiny lines that fanned out from the corners of his eyes. Against a pale blue linen shirt that emphasized the set of his large expanse of shoulder, the lean tanned face and shiny black hair provided a startling contrast.

"I thought you would like to know what I decided to do about your brother," he said, stopping to squash his cigarette under the heel of his boot.

Maile stared at him as he bent to pick up the butt, eyes round with apprehension. She held her breath, fearing he would say that he had changed his mind and was now fully prepared to prosecute Bryan for embezzlement.

"Well?" she demanded, letting out her pent-up breath in a rush.

"Oh, you *are* interested," he remarked dryly. "The way you rushed off this afternoon, I had the distinct impression that you didn't care."

Frowning with puzzlement, Maile racked her brain to recall what had been said between them that afternoon, but could not remember him mentioning Bryan except to threaten he would blacken his professional reputation unless she acquiesced to his outrageous demands. "You never said anything about Bryan," she whispered, her tone just a hairbreadth from being accusatory.

"You might not have heard me—as I recall you did a

lot of daydreaming—but I did say that I wanted to discuss something with you that concerned him." Taking her arm, Jake urged her across the street and away from the residential district.

Had he? Maile honestly could not remember. "Well, I *am* interested, so tell me now."

A frown cut into his wide brow, and he stared down at her thoughtfully, giving Maile the disturbing impression that whatever he had decided to do about Bryan, it was not good.

Seeing her thoughts so clearly revealed on her face, Jake back-pedaled, and instead of using Bryan's precarious position to threaten her into bending to his will, he proposed that they make a trade.

"A trade?" she asked warily, frowning at the smile that curved Jake's mouth. "What sort of trade?"

"It's clear that you want nothing to do with me, Maile," he said quietly, his tone rueful. "I've been thinking. I'll let you off the hook, give your brother a job somewhere in the corporation—if, in return, I can supervise the races and—"

"Not on your life!" Jerking her arm free of his hold, she turned to face him, her hands locked together tightly in an effort to keep the anger smoldering behind her green eyes from boiling over. She took a deep breath, fighting for calm, and then added in a quieter tone, "I will not have you interfering in the operation of Mike's speedway, even if I have to—" She had meant to say that she would rather suffer through a few miserable dates with him when Jake rudely interrupted her, his voice grating.

"Oh, so it's *Mike's* speedway, is it?" His jawline visibly hardened. "You forget that I own thirty percent of the rotten business." He leaned toward her, and she saw the ill-repressed anger lurking in the depths of his blue eyes. "And *that*, lover, gives me a certain authority.

"But I won't lean on you—not yet," he added, straightening, shrugging inside his Levi's jacket. "First, let me tell you a little bit about Arthur and what your devil's playground can do to him."

Arthur. The name echoed in her mind. Again he had said Arthur, not David. Maile's heart sang with relief, and she was able to smile as he talked about his mysterious errant nephew whose name was *not* David. Unconsciously she blocked out his words, listening only to the soft huskiness of his voice, and was startled out of her wits when he turned and grasped her arms.

"I don't want to lean on you, Maile, but I won't let even you get in my way!"

Maile glanced upward to his face, casting about in her mind for a satisfactory answer, and failing. She compressed her lips. "I wish you wouldn't try to make your problems mine, Mr. Weston," she said quietly but firmly. "Now, you can believe me or not, that is your prerogative, but I do *not* know your nephew."

Jake smiled sardonically. As he stared into her frustrated expression, he wondered at his refusal to believe her. The helpless look in her eyes tugged at his heart, but he remembered another pair of lovely green eyes looking at him in just that way, and he felt as though a cold hand had reached into his guts and was squeezing the breath from him.

"I'm not in the habit of repeating myself, but I'll make an exception this time. I'm warning you: if you insist on encouraging Arthur in this insane notion he has of racing, you'll regret it—I'll see that you do."

"What do you mean?" If anyone was a candidate for the

77

booby hatch, it was this strange man who clung tenaciously to his misconception that she knew his nephew.

"It means that I will do anything I have to to keep him from lousing up his life, even if it means mowing *you* under." His hands dropped away as though he could no longer bear to touch her.

Maile's anger took strong root, driving away her fear of him. She knew exactly what he meant. Obsessed with keeping his nephew from racing, he would not hesitate to bring legal action against her and the speedway, even if closing it meant he would throw several innocent people out of work. But would he care? No! After all, they were all strangers to him. All *he* cared about was winning in the battle he was fighting with his wayward nephew.

A shudder tore through her body as she scanned the tall pantherish figure and arrogant face. This is the man I feel so strongly about, she told herself in a silent, mocking voice. This cold, unfeeling, arrogant— She broke off her angry train of thought and took a deep breath to chase away tears that were threateningly close.

"I suppose you think that by closing me down, you will stifle your nephew's desire to race," she taunted quietly, her temper tightly reined. "And what else will you do, Mr. Weston, to make the poor kid dance to your tune?" She forced a wry smile. "It's no wonder the boy is so eager to grow up and leave your guardianship!"

"And just what is that supposed to mean?" he demanded, the corners of his sensuous mouth hardening in anger.

"Simply this, Mr. Weston," her voice was quieter still, the fight slowly leaving her. "You are one of the most dictatorial and unpleasant men I've ever had the misfortune to meet. I'm willing to bet that you order the poor kid around and bully him into obeying you, deceiving

78

yourself while telling *him* that everything you do is for his own good." She laughed sarcastically. "Deliver me from people who hide their meddling under the guise of doing good for others!" She turned to go, but was stopped by his hand coming down hard on her shoulder.

"How dare you say such a thing!" He bent further, glaring into her overbright eyes. "Arthur and I had a good relationship until he got this damned bug about racing. Your boyfriend"—he spat out the word as though it were obscene—"didn't help any by giving him a free pass to his damned speedway."

"Mike—" She started to defend him by saying that Mike had generously handed out the free passes to any youngster who called or wrote in for them, but before she could get the words said, he added in an extremely hateful voice, "And now, you. Sight unseen, or so you tell me, you are determined to help him defy me."

The reins on Maile's temper began to fray. "If you cannot keep your house in order, Mr. Weston, don't blame *me* for it." Her tone then became flippant. "You were probably having problems with him before either Mike or I came along," she tossed off carelessly, relief in knowing that David was not his nephew being the controlling emotion. She liked David and somehow could not picture him being related to someone like Jake Weston.

"Look who's talking about keeping one's house in order!" he jeered.

He was referring to Bryan and the missing money, of course. In his mind Bryan would always be a thief. Her Achilles' heel had been wounded; she had no words with which to defend herself.

"I don't think we have anything more to discuss, Mr.

Weston. Good night!" Bowing her head she started back to her house.

He caught up to her easily, and grabbed her by the arm, not ungently. Maile tried to free herself but his hold, light though it was, was unbreakable.

"Since I came all this way to talk to you, it is up to me to decide when our meeting will be over." His voice was like ice as he continued. "Because you have nothing further to say to me, it doesn't necessarily follow that I have nothing further to say to you, Maile Riordan."

Maile gritted her teeth in exasperation. "Since I'm not one of your poor, unfortunate employees, Mr. Weston, I am not obligated to listen to you."

"Damn you, woman, do you have to be so stubborn?"

"Stubborn?" She forced a dry, taunting laugh. "Which one of us insists on blaming the other for *his* problems, Mr. Weston?" she mocked, yanking her arm out of his grip. "Now, as I said, we have nothing further to discuss."

A flicker of uncertainty eased the angry set of his features, and suddenly he smiled. "You're right. . . . I am the stubborn one . . . and I'm determined to talk to you." He hooked his arm through hers, gently pulling her toward him. "Come then, little feisty kitten, buy me a cup of coffee, and let's talk sensibly. I promise not to antagonize you further."

Maile glared up at him in helpless, impotent anger. She shook her head, wondering if she would ever understand him. She started walking back to the house, her mind churning with senseless thoughts. What more did they have to talk about? Was he going to persist with his foolish idea that she *knew* his nephew and, therefore, was lying to him? Not that she cared, she told herself hastily, but why didn't he believe she was telling the truth?

Jake took the key from her after Maile took it from its hiding place. He opened the door. As he stepped into the house behind her she began to wonder how he saw her humble home.

Except for the lamps, which she had bought at an auction, the furniture in this room consisted of odds and ends that Mike had had in his apartment. Maile had sold the furniture that she and Bryan had grown up with to help pay Bryan's tuition so that he could attend school full-time. The sofa—brown-striped velvet—had come first, she remembered with a nostalgic pang. Mike told her it was just taking up room in his apartment, but she had known it was because he hated her shabby green sofa with the broken springs and lumpy cushions. The brown easy chair and matching rectangular ottoman had come next because Mike had bought a billiard table and needed room for that. The bookcase, replete with books, had been the next to leave Mike's home shortly before he had shown up with a sheepish grin and a suitcase and informed her that he had been evicted and needed a place to stay "for a few days only."

"About that coffee?" Jake nudged her, shrewdly interrupting her nostalgic thoughts.

Maile moved away from that warm hand that had sent an electric shock trailing up her spine, anxiously seeking the safety of her kitchen. After the exchange of the past few minutes she had no real wish to share even a measly cup of coffee with him, but it was apparent he would not leave before he said what he had come to say. So be it! she thought furiously as she plugged in the coffeepot. One cup of coffee, and then out he went!

In her preoccupation Maile did not notice that Jake had not returned her house key. He stood in the middle of the room, smiling as he slipped the key into the pocket of his jeans before following her into the kitchen.

"You move around this place as though you really know what you're doing," he teased as he came up behind her.

Smiling, Maile set a plate of homemade cookies on a tray beside their two cups of coffee. "You'd be surprised at what I know," she countered ingenuously as she squeezed past him to get to the refrigerator for the cream.

"Would I, now?" he murmured, cocking one dark, mocking brow. Smiling, he leaned against the sink counter and watched her, his eyes half concealed behind heavily fringed lids.

Angered at what she took to be a sex-oriented challenge and the arrogance he exhibited in his indolent stance, Maile drew herself up and replied in the coldest tone she could muster, "Probably not. I doubt there are any surprises left for a man of your . . . experience." She took napkins from the cupboard above her and slapped them down beside his cup.

"You're right, honey. I'm as jaded as that look in your eyes." He laughed softly, deeply, before adding in an unnervingly complacent tone, "But we didn't come here to investigate my fall to turpitude.

"I intend to offer your brother a job in my Seattle operations." He waited a moment, and when Maile did not comment, he continued. "He'll be in the purchasing operation, but he won't be in a position to disburse any money. I hope you can understand that I cannot place him in a position with financial responsibility again."

Maile longed to ask why, all of a sudden, he was so concerned with gaining her approval, but remembered in time that old adage about not looking a gift horse in the mouth, and simply nodded.

"*Thank you, Jake,*" he said with a grim twist of his mouth.

"On behalf of Bryan, thank you, Mr. Weston."

"Is that all I get for my generosity?" His tone was soft, but the expression in his eyes was hard and left no doubt as to the type of gratuity he might expect for his so-called generosity.

Go to him! cried every tingly fiber in her body, but *Stay!* cautioned her fearful mind and heart. Maile trembled inwardly; her fragile heart seemed to contract. It should be the easiest thing to walk across the room to where he stood, go right into his arms, and answer his question with a kiss. But she couldn't. Though the distance that separated them was not great, Maile could not gap it. Once she made that trip across to him, there would be no turning back, and she could not take the first step.

"I'll have Bryan drop by and give you his thanks personally," she snapped, hiding behind simulated anger to mask her true feelings.

"He's not my type," Jake countered with a laugh.

"And neither am I!"

"My dear girl," he murmured, "you might allow me to be the judge of that." And then he was strolling with indolent grace across the room, and Maile was stepping back in an effort to avoid him.

But there was no place to go. Her back was against the refrigerator, and he was still advancing. His eyes danced with some inner sense of—what? Amusement? Or was that cold determination? Or was it just out-and-out male confidence? Maile did not know. She knew only that she was trapped.

What could she do? Scream? That would only bring some of her neighbors and lead to unpleasant scenes. And this obnoxiously confident man would no doubt stand there feigning innocence, leaving her to try to explain her screams.

"What's the matter, Chicken Little, no place to run?" His hand gripped her chin, turning her face up to his. He smiled crookedly, his eyes intent on her quivering lips. "You're trembling, Maile," he whispered, his voice surprising her with its ring of concern. "You're not cold, are you?"

His arms went around her even as she was thinking to reach up her fists to hold him at bay. "Oh, Maile." He breathed huskily against her brow as his lips trailed a fiery path across it. "You're so beautiful," he murmured, bringing her closer to him. Then, suddenly, his mouth was on hers—savage, seeking, exploring, roughly coaxing her into responding; and she could taste whiskey in that kiss, she thought distractedly. Seeking, deftly caressing, his hands moved over her back and shoulders; took hold of her buttocks and pressed her closer to the warm, hard length of him.

A wave of sensation swept through her limbs, leaving her enervated and clinging to him. Her arms went around his neck, her fingers involuntarily curling into the sensual thickness of the hair that matted at his nape.

His hand moved up, his fingers tangled in her hair, bunching it against her neck. "Oh, Maile, I want you so." Maile shivered at the impassioned whisper, his voice sounding unnaturally low. With a groan coming deep from his chest, he buried his head under her chin, his mouth moist and warm against the jerky pulse at her

84

throat. "Maile," he breathed, moving his mouth up the column of her neck. "Oh, Maile!"

Just as his mouth began moving seductively over hers, she felt an arm go under her knees; then she was being cradled against his heaving chest and he was walking with rapid, confident steps toward her bedroom.

From somewhere in her mind came a nagging little voice that told her he might want her, but he would never love her. He would only satisfy a desire with her that he could just as easily satisfy with any other woman. And that was not what she wanted. Not for her a one-night stand; Maile Riordan wanted *forever,* or nothing at all!

That taunting little voice within had its effect, and Maile began to struggle again, frustratedly aware she was no match for his superior strength, yet determined to fight him off. She pushed desperately against his chest, but it was like trying to move a brick wall.

"Stop! Oh, please stop!" she cried hoarsely, still pushing against that brick wall to release herself from his gentle, yet firm, embrace.

"It's too late to stop, Maile," he whispered almost incoherently against her mouth.

Panic rose like bile to her throat as she felt herself being placed in the center of the bed. Then Jake's weight was pressing her down, demanding submission with arms that held her immobile against him, lips that sent small rivulets of fire coursing through her veins despite a desperate resolve not to let this man arouse her to passion.

No, it isn't! Maile thought. Gasping for breath, she fought as hard against him as she fought against a heady urge to surrender to him.

"Don't fight me, Maile," he whispered fiercely, nibbling lightly on her ear while his hands undid the buttons of her blouse and pushed the flimsy silk off her shoulders. At some point he had removed his shirt and now he flung it over his shoulder, becoming more intent on his purpose. His arms tightened around her again, conquering her weak opposition with arrogant confidence and a powerful physique that kept her pinned beneath him.

Fleetingly she wondered what had ever possessed her to trust this man in her house, then she concentrated all her force to push him off her.

For a moment he slacked off, his passion-clouded eyes silently questioning her as they lingered on her flushed face. Then his lips curved, but it wasn't a smile.

"C'mon, Maile, don't play the little innocent with me," he mocked hatefully, a marauding finger playing with a tautened nipple through the flesh-colored tricot of her skimpy bra.

His taunt served to increase her desire to push him away. Laughing, he pinned her down, his hands trapping her flailing arms against her sides, one long, muscular leg thrown over both of hers to keep her quiet.

"It's not like you haven't been with men before," he muttered, a definite slur in his tone.

Maile's bruised lips parted in a gasp. She closed her eyes tightly in an effort to stem the threatened tide. But it was no use. Hot stinging tears flooded her eyes and trailed down her cheeks. "Only wi-with Mike," she faltered. "And I loved him." Her breath caught, and for a moment she could not continue. But she remembered Mike's sweet and loving seduction and somehow Jake's words had made it seem sordid and dirty.

"And he loved me," she whispered tearfully, wiping the tears from her face by moving her head from side to side on the pillow. "And . . . we—we were going to be m-m-married, but he g-g-got ki—killed!" Biting hard on her quivering lower lip, she turned her face into her pillow and muffled her sobs against its downy softness.

"Oh, God!" he muttered thickly. In the next instant she was alone in the bed. Muttering under his breath, Jake threw on his shirt. Tucking the shirt angrily into his jeans, he pulled up the zipper and fastened the snap at his waist, mumbling an oath under his breath.

Quickly, if shakily, Maile rearranged her clothes over her trembling form, redoing the buttons of her blouse with trembling fingers. "It's not like you haven't been with men before. . . ." The insult echoed hatefully in her brain and, with a shuddering breath, she gave Jake her back, hugging her pillow for what little comfort it gave her. She sniffed. Lord, how could he be so hateful!

"Maile, I—" Her tears had disarmed him; he looked wretched, but Maile did not see it with her face pressed to the pillow. He reached out, touching her only with the tips of his fingers.

"Don't touch me!" She sprang to the floor on the other side of the bed, her cheeks still flooded with color, her eyes overbright from crying. Whatever else he said or did, she would never forgive him for what he had said to her.

For a moment they stood facing each other across the tumbled, satin-covered battleground. His eyes as they went over her flushed face still held a glimmer of desire, but Maile met that sensuous look with an expression of intense dislike.

Jake muttered something under his breath, and started around the bed only to stop when he saw her shrinking away.

"Stay away from me, Jake," she ordered coldly, her fists

clenching at her sides. "Don't you ever come near me again!"

Shamelessly he retreated. "All right," he said in a voice that had gone as soft as sin. "If that's the way you want it, I'll go now. But I'm coming back." His voice was softer yet, and more than a little dangerous.

Still smarting from his earlier insult, Maile lifted her chin fractionally, her eyes glittering with disdain. "Not here, you're not," she retorted, indicating the bed with a nod of her disheveled head. A curling tendril fell across her eyes, and she pushed it back angrily.

Jake's lips twitched briefly. "No, of course not. At least —not until you ask me." His voice was confident, as though he knew it would be only hours before Maile would be on the phone calling him back.

"In that case, *Mister* Weston," she said frigidly, "I wouldn't hold my breath with anticipation."

His eyes went over her slowly as though they were cataloging every minute detail that made her Maile Riordan, and when he finally spoke, it was in that same softly tantalizing voice. "I won't," he said. With a mocking farewell salute he moved out of her bedroom, nonchalance in every stride. His fingers reached into his pocket for her key, and he smiled as he pulled it out, turning to face her.

"Here," he said, tossing her the key. "I wouldn't want you to lose any sleep worrying that at any time, day or night, I'd be able to let myself into your home."

Maile stared blankly at her key, her mind unable to function beyond feeling a certain relief in seeing him gone. Slowly her fingers closed over her key.

Forcing her quivering legs to move, she crossed the room after she'd heard Jake close the front door and went into the front room. She stared at the closed door, her mind churning with recollection of all that had happened since she had opened it to Jake at eight. Shuddering with feeling, she hurried across the room and threw home the bolt, not satisfied until she had tried to open the door herself to make certain that it was properly locked. Only then did she feel secure enough to return to her bed.

CHAPTER 5

In the weeks that followed, Jake turned up several times at Maile's house, but he very carefully avoided talk of the speedway *or* his nephew, and he kept his distance. Maile, fully aware of her strong feelings for him, managed to steel herself against these visits, and was successful, she thought, at keeping her emotions perfectly under control.

But though he made no move toward her, Maile sensed he was just biding his time, lulling her into a false sense of security. She found it, therefore, infinitely safer to be with him only in restaurants or outside her house, walking about Watsonville or just sitting on her porch talking. Indeed, she was throwing herself into the task of reopening the speedway with such single-minded dedication that she had no time to worry about how easily Jake was maneuvering himself into her life. He was charming and very attentive without being obtrusive. He brought her flowers; the nights she was working late, he took her dinner at the boutique. On weekends he arrived early at the speedway and took her to lunch, then left her to do heaven only knew what until it was time for her to go home. He never once tried to intrude into the operation of the speedway. Indeed, he never even stayed to watch the races.

One evening Maile heard the roar of a car coming to a stop outside her house as she was fixing her dinner. She stopped, set down knife and celery stalk, and hurried to the window of the front room, her heart pounding, expecting to see Jake sauntering up the drive.

"David." She sagged with disappointment and felt very much like crying. It was then that the truth struck her: She was hopelessly in love with Jake Weston! Her heart fluttered like a winged thing in her breast, and for a moment, she didn't know what to do, what to think.

In the next instant all thought of Jake Weston fled as she opened the door to find David scowling behind it.

"Something wrong?" she asked, stepping aside to let him come in. He didn't reply; if anything, his scowl deepened.

As Maile closed the door David turned to face her, his eyes dark with anger.

"Maile, didn't you tell Mike's lawyer that it was okay for me to use the speedway?" She nodded. "Then why the hell do you suppose he sent me this?" he demanded, holding out a crumpled envelope. Maile took it, frowning with confusion as she took the letter and started to read it. Except for saying David would be using the track off and on, she had not mentioned him the other times she had spoken with Jim Boyden.

Yet, here was a letter supposedly written on her behalf telling David that letting him use the track was an inconvenience to its new owner. She looked up from the letter. "When did you get this?"

"Yesterday." His anger seemed to be dissipating. "I don't understand it, Maile. First, you tell me that you're going to talk to this guy . . . and then I get that."

Maile studied the letter. Though Boyden's signature was almost illegible, it was no doubt his; she had seen it often enough to know it was. But the letter itself bothered her—it was typed on a plain sheet, not the fancy letterhead Jim used. And it didn't mention David by name. . . .

"David, I didn't tell Jim that having you around the track was a nuisance to me." She tapped the letter with her finger, frowning in thought. "I really don't know where he got the notion to say that I did."

The brown eyes suddenly sparkled, and sought her eyes as the youthful lips spread in smile. "*You.*" He chuckled, a deep from-the-belly chuckle. "I should've known!"

Maile was stunned by the swiftness of his action, and could do nothing but stand rigid in his arms as they went around her in a bear hug.

"Oh, Maile, you adorable lovely girl!" Unashamedly he bent and kissed her on the cheek. "You wouldn't want to adopt me, would you?" he teased hopefully.

"No." She laughed nervously, pushing away from him.

"Why not?" he shot at her, grinning. "Think the neighbors would gossip?" he added, quirking a mocking brow.

Maile choked back a retort that would not only have embarrassed her but would also have put the audacious young man in his place. "I was just about to fix a salad for dinner. Would you like some, or a sandwich?"

"Only something to drink."

"Coke or orange juice?"

"I was thinking of something a little stronger, but I'll settle for a Coke."

Grateful for something to do, Maile hurried into the

kitchen. She finished making her salad, put it and a Coke on a tray, and went back to the living room to find David prowling around the room looking at Mike's trophies and pictures.

"He was good, wasn't he?" David asked, turning to take his drink.

Maile nodded. She sat on Mike's chair, quietly sipping her coffee, her salad forgotten for the moment. Mike had always been the best he could be, no matter what he did. She smiled as she watched David take down a trophy from the shelf Bryan had built for her to display all of Mike's treasures. He fondled it gently, a strange expression on his narrow face.

"Mike won that one when he was twenty," she explained as he replaced the trophy between two others.

"Yeah, I know." In a voice thick with emotion he ticked off the date and race at which Mike had won each prize while Maile listened in stunned silence. When he was done, he sat down on the sofa and finished his drink in moody silence.

What was he thinking? Maile wondered as he sat there staring at Mike's collection. Was he imagining himself in Mike's place, winning races and girls, his reputation with both preceding him at every track?

For the first time in months Maile felt the pangs of jealousy she had experienced each time she had seen girls throwing themselves at Mike. She shook her head and glanced out the window in discomfort.

For a while she had been with Mike when he was on the Grand Prix circuit. It had been a time of enlightenment for her; it had taught her a lot about men. She had at first been shocked out of her old-fashioned mind to see the ease with which some of the drivers discarded their women and immediately began to pursue others. And Mike, she had heard, was like all the others, if not worse. Maile had tried not to believe the rumors, but had kept her guard up. When she began to suspect that Mike was tiring of her, she had run home to Bryan. Mike had followed in her wake, missing an important race. . . .

Sadly she wrenched her mind away to other thoughts.

"Do you want another drink?" she asked, gathering her things to take back to the kitchen.

"If you don't mind, I'd like another drink."

"How about some cookies?" she called out.

"Are they homemade?" came the reply in a hopeful voice.

"Of course! Oatmeal."

"Bring them out. They're my favorite."

Smiling, Maile returned to the living room with the cookies and another drink for him. She set her tray down beside him and moved back to Mike's chair.

"Did you really make these?" he asked, his tone doubtful.

"Of course I did."

"Mmm. Beauty and culinary expert rolled into one," he teased, adding, "you'd make a guy a wonderful aunt. Are you sure you don't want to adopt me?"

"I'm certain." She laughed. "You want the speedway owner to adopt you, not me," she accused.

Laughing, he prompted her to tell him about the places she and Mike had seen when they were on the circuit. In turn he told her a little—a precious little—about his life. As he talked, it struck her that he was being very cagey. Each time she asked a question that would inevitably lead to her discovering more about his family, he changed the subject.

94

"You're pretty close-mouthed about your relatives, aren't you?" she asked, her tone edged with exasperation.

He shrugged dismissively. "There's nothing to say about them, Maile." As he smiled she had a fleeting impression that he looked like someone she knew. Was it Mike? She stared openly at his features, dissecting them carefully, and decided that, except for the tawny hair, he did not resemble Mike Sloan at all. He looked more like . . . who? The resemblance was so fleeting, so vague, it escaped her completely, frustrating her.

"It's getting late, David," she said, leaving her chair to show him to the door. "If I don't get my full eight hours, I'll be an absolute wreck in the morning."

"Speaking of wrecks," he said, eyes sparkling with mischief. "Want to try your car against mine sometime?"

"I don't race," she said swiftly. "I'm like that little old lady from Pasadena who drives her car only on Sundays, and then only to church and back. I drive mine only to and from work, and very carefully. It was a present from Mike, you understand. . . ."

"Yes, Maile," he said, and he laughed a strong, mocking sort of laugh that tickled her memory with its resemblance to someone else's. He gave her no time to analyze that faint resemblance, adding in a sweetly challenging voice, "I know what it is, Maile. You're afraid that I can beat you, so you don't even want to try me."

"Get out of here," she ordered in a mock furious tone, pushing him out the door.

"Can I come see you tomorrow?"

"I'm busy tomorrow, Dave. But why don't you come to the speedway in the afternoon? I have to talk to a few of Mike's friends about some of the things I need to do before it opens, and they promised to meet me there about two tomorrow."

"Hey, that would be great!" And he bounded off her porch, letting loose one of his habitual rebel yells as he ran to his car.

"Good night, Maile, see you tomorrow!" he called out as he opened the door of his car.

"Night, Dave." She leaned against the door, watching him as he climbed into his car and drove away. As the red taillights faded out of sight Maile closed the door, this time making double sure that she locked it.

She awoke to the sound of knuckles pounding on her door. Groggily she threw off her covers and turned to the clock on her nightstand. Seven o'clock! Who in the world could be knocking on her door on a Saturday at seven in the morning?

Muttering under her breath, she slipped into her robe and went to the door, determined to tell whoever had had the nerve to wake her that he or she should go away and come back in three or four hours.

But when she opened the door, all thought of sending away her early-morning visitor left her.

"Jake!" Ah, so much feeling had been put into his name. Too late she realized she had forgotten cardinal rule number one: Do not let Jake Weston know how you feel about him.

Sunlight gleamed on his bare head, fully illuminating his arrogant features. The dark tan of his skin made his blue eyes appear an unstable turquoise. "Good morning, Miss Riordan," he mocked.

His gaze held hers as she unconsciously reached up to smooth back her sleep-tumbled hair. As she did so, the front of her robe gaped, exposing to his watchful eyes the deep valley between her breasts as well as the gentle swell of one breast. It was a moment before she became aware of the way his hooded gaze traveled from her face to the shadowed cleft between her breasts.

Maile stirred restlessly, as aware of her disheveled state as she was of the masculinity emanating from the man facing her. "Would you like to come in?" She squirmed mentally, her voice had been too low—and too damned husky!

Jake walked in, smiling, and went straight to Mike's chair. "I thought I'd let you cook me breakfast," he said as he made himself comfortable in the chair. He chuckled hoarsely. "Unless, of course, you have something better to offer?"

Maile choked back a gasp. He was through waiting, and his next words confirmed it.

"I want you, Maile."

She stepped back, nervously clutching the front of her robe. She tried not to look at the long athletic legs of the man who was striding, smiling, across the room to her; and she tried to put on a courageous act, but failed. Her hands trembled at her throat, and there was no way she could stop them from doing so.

"Why are you shaking, Maile?" came his voice, soft and just a little bit amused.

"Who's shaking?" she demanded tremulously, taking another step backward.

"You are." Hands jaded with experience reached out and gently pried her hands away from her robe. "And it's not that you're cold. Good God, it must be ninety in here!" His hands went to her face, touching it gently, then wound their way to the easily aroused nape of her neck. "And you haven't just come out of the shower," he whispered, his voice unnervingly low and husky, "so I can only assume that you keep the heat up because you sleep in the raw."

Maile choked on his words, and tried to move away, to break the spell that devil was casting on her, but the hand on her back curled around her neck, holding her.

"Don't be frightened, baby. I said I want you. I did not say I was going to do anything about it just now." His deep, seductive chuckle was irritating in its triumph. "I'll wait for an invitation." It had been a mistake to let him in. But why was she standing here, transfixed beneath his caressing hands? Why didn't she speak up, demand that he leave?

Hands that had been scorching a path from her neck to her waist finally settled on her hips. Smiling lazily, Jake bent toward her until she could feel that rapid come-and-go of his breath warmly fanning her lips.

"Jake, no. . . ."

The pressure of his mouth on hers was firm, commanding, urging a pliancy from her lips. When at last her mouth responded to his kiss, his mouth moved moistly over hers, consuming, demanding, drawing her into a kiss that was meant to rob her of her senses.

"Are you ready to invite me to your bed?"

Though her senses were spinning wildly with each caress of his experienced hands, Maile could only shake her head. But even as she refused, she sought his lips, her hands moving over his chest, fingers exploring, teasing, coming to a stop in the mass of crisp black hair showing through the opening of his silk shirt. She felt him shudder and, misunderstanding his reaction, stilled her fingers.

"Don't back off," he murmured against the curve of her mouth.

98

Maile was confused. She had made no move to disengage herself from his arms. Answering a strange need within her, her fingers moved up, tugging at the buttons of his shirt until the two fronts were apart. Shyly her hands slid over the hard flesh of his stomach and around to the flexing muscles of his back.

"That's right, honey," he murmured, covering her closed eyes, her cheeks, her mouth, with tiny little kisses that left her breathless.

Every instinct told her to escape now, or it would be too late, yet every nerve in her body tingled with anticipation of what was going to happen between them.

"Maile?" he whispered, his voice thick with the urgency of his desire. "Maile?"

Maile stiffened and looked up into his hooded gaze, her eyes widening in surprise as he pressed her hips firmly against his muscular thighs, making her embarrassingly aware of his growing passion.

"No, Jake, please. Let me go," she protested weakly when his hands gently untied the sash and parted her robe, revealing the beauty of her body to him. She shivered as his hands wandered persuasively around her slender waist and across her taut stomach. His knee spread her thighs and he pressed himself against her, making her sharply aware of his impatience.

She tried to push at his chest, only to find that her fingers would rather twine themselves in the great mass of matted black hair they found there.

"Oh, Maile, you don't know what you do to me!" With a strangled moan he swung her up into his arms and carried her into her bedroom. Very gently he placed her on the bed, and then followed her down.

Slowly, tentatively, he folded her into his arms, molding

her pliant flesh against his male hardness. Maile was only dimly aware of the fact that he was wearing jeans that were harsh against her thighs. His mouth was finding all the erotic areas along her neck and throat, teasing them, making her shudder with desire. There wasn't an inch of her body that did not feel the warmth of those experienced hands.

"Maile!" His voice seemed to be forced from deep within his chest. Hands that increased the fire in her blood caressed her breasts, trailed with tantalizing slowness across her taut stomach, moving over downy territory to the sensitive inner part of her thighs. Her breath caught as his warm fingers stole into the core of her desire. A soft moan escaped her, muffled against the lips that seared the corner of her mouth.

"You can't stay cold to me forever, Maile," he breathed, trailing his lips down the column of her neck to her breasts. She felt his tongue lick against a nipple, felt it treacherously stiffen under his command, betraying the response she was still reluctant to admit.

"Maile?" he groaned, capturing the nipple between his strong teeth, gently pressing down on it.

Unconsciously she arched her body, instinctively seeking fulfillment from the male frame stretched out beside her.

Surrender trembled on her lips. "Oh, Jake," she breathed, "please don't tease!"

"Are you asking me to love you, Maile?"

"God help me, yes!"

Without moving his mouth from hers, Jake reached down to remove his jeans, flinging them to the floor. He moved very slowly over her, prolonging the sweet torment, teasing her with light kisses that were rained over her face and breasts until Maile felt like screaming. In some dim part of her mind she wondered if he was trying to drive her crazy.

Urgent fingers dug into the rippling muscles of his back in desperation, pressing him to her, willing him to appease the hunger that was like an engulfing ball of fire centered in her abdomen. She arched her body beneath his, inviting, demanding, while her lips moved under his, begging, "Please, Jake, please love me!"

A small inarticulate sound bubbled up between their merging mouths as flesh melted into flesh and she experienced the familiar intrusion into her body. Gentle at first—once he was sure of her—Jake moved rhythmically with purpose, flooding her body with sensations all but forgotten. She heard his gasping ragged breathing as he took them up, up, up, to the peak of ecstasy. And then they were floating downward, drifting like a leaf in the wind. . . .

Maile lay quietly in the warm cocoon of his muscular arms, a dreamy, satisfied smile on her lips. A pleasant, debilitating weakness had attacked her limbs, and she was content to remain where she was, enjoying the warmth and security of the male body pressed to hers.

"Ah, Maile," his husky voice said in her ear. "I could stay here with you forever."

Encouraged by the emotion she heard in his voice, Maile stretched with feline grace and turned to look up at him.

"I love you, Jake," she confessed with unveiled joy in her voice. "I love you," she repeated, no longer caring about her pride, hunger expressed in the tiny kisses she pressed upon his face.

"And I love you," he said finally; but his tone held no

conviction. Or was it that she was looking for trouble? Maile did not know. She knew only that there had been too much delay between her confession and his response.

"Where are you going?" he growled as she rolled away from him.

"To make some coffee," she replied quietly. She needed to get away from him—to think. He watched her gently swinging hips as she walked away from him; then he slid out of bed, climbed into his jeans, and followed her.

"Maile?" He came up behind her as she was struggling into her robe, sliding his hands around her waist, crossing them in front to cup her breasts. "Mmm. . . ." Sliding her hair away from her neck with his chin, he pressed his mouth against the cool skin. "Maile, you're not feeling bad about what just happened between us, are you?" And when she did not answer, he pulled her against him. A groan seemed to come from somewhere deep in his chest. In the next instant Maile found herself being swung around to face him.

"You do regret it, don't you?" he demanded in a voice that crackled with intensity, echoing in the empty house. Narrowed and ice-cold, his eyes moved over her face, searching her impassive expression. Light streaming in through the window fell on his expression, accentuating the angles of his face, deepening his jawline and hardening his mouth with a grimness that gave it a cruel look. "Answer me, damn you!"

Maile drew a calming breath. "Yes, I suppose I do," she whispered. Her lips began to tremble, and she couldn't control them. She turned her face away, cursing herself for being affected so disastrously by this man.

Sighing, he drew her to him and kissed her. "Ah, Maile"—he mocked, but gently—"you're old-fashioned enough to think you have to be *in* love before you *make* love, and I understand your feeling that way—"

"But?" she challenged, battling against a wave of hot shame that flooded her body as she recalled her uninhibited response to his lovemaking.

He raked a hand through his tousled hair, an expression of indecision marring his handsome features. "It's different for a man, Maile. A man doesn't fall in love quite as easily as a woman."

Maile winced inwardly and moved out of his arms. She looked up at him with resentment. She had lain in his arms, felt the love expressed by his hungry body, and answered its call with a hunger of her own. He had made rainbows explode in her mind. Her lips curved down ruefully. He had given her wings, and then taken away the sky. . . .

Dazedly, she moved away from him, her eyes glued to the door, freedom beckoning just on the other side. She firmed her backbone, and moved toward the door only to be stopped by his hand on her wrist.

"Come back here, Maile," he murmured, drawing her to him, hugging her so hard that Maile's breath came out in a gasp.

"I wasn't saying I don't love you, Maile . . . only that it's such a new and—well, *frightening* experience for me, I need time. . . ."

Forcing feeling into her leadened limbs, Maile pushed away from him and went into the kitchen, busying her trembling hands with making the coffee, keeping her thoughts centered on that menial chore. Mechanically she took the coffeepot and filled it with water, then dropped the coffee grounds into the basket and plugged it in. She stood with her arms folded across her breasts, staring at the pot as it started to perk. He did *not* love her. With a sickening rush of despair she saw what a fool she had been to think that he ever would. A sob caught in her throat, and she swallowed hard, clenching her teeth in an effort to stem the hot stinging tears waiting to fall.

A step, soft yet purposeful, came from behind her, but she kept her eyes riveted to the coffeepot, her arms over her breasts, hands balled into fists.

"Give me time, Maile," Jake begged in a husky whisper, circling her stiff shoulders with his arms, drawing her rigid form against his broad chest. "I feel love for you, Maile, but I need time to explore my feelings."

Lust is what you feel, she thought viciously, trying to stop herself from melting against him. His nearness made her breath come in ragged gasps; his touch set her body on fire. It would not take him too much time to have her dependent upon him for the very air she breathed. And being the sort of man he was, he would wield his power over her indiscriminately, molding her to suit his whims. She would end hating them both.

"A little bit of time, honey," he said, turning her around in his arms, "to get used to the idea of belonging to you," he whispered, taking her silence as a sign of submission. He gathered her gently to him, holding her head against his chest with one hand, which was roughly smoothing her hair. The erratic hammering of his heart came as a surprise to her. She risked a glance at him through a strand of hair, and found him frowning.

"I need you, Maile," he murmured against her brow. "And you need me, too, and you know it."

Yes, but for how long? Maile asked herself. Would he need her as long as she would need him? No. He would not. He could not. She smiled with grim amusement. He was more like Bryan than he would care to discover. Like Bryan, he was afraid to commit himself to just one woman. What had been his words? "It's different for a man. . . ."

Maile tightened her jaw. She could not let him go. She would not. She would give him time. Somehow, in some way, she would make him love her alone.

"I won't be your mistress, Jake." She choked, recoiling from the thought and from his arms, turning her back to him. "I do not need a man that badly."

"I never said I want you for my mistress," he mumbled, moving against her, his hands reaching out to caress the curve of her hip. "In fact, I would never insult you by suggesting such a thing," he added in a loverlike whisper as he pressed his face into the mass of hair hanging to her shoulder. "Just be my love. . . ."

Her breath caught in her throat even as she swayed closer to him. A tingling warmth spread its way down from the gentle caress of his hands and lips. Maile knew she should resist, yet she could not; she seemed rooted to the spot, her body under the spell of those experienced hands.

"What do you say, Maile?"

His mouth moved urgently across the length of her neck, over her cheek, to settle over the throbbing pulse at her temple. He held her tightly against him until some of her rigidity faded; slowly he relaxed his hold, then deftly turned her around in his arms.

"Maile?"

"Yes," she whispered faintly, shivering as she wondered what kind of purgatory she was committing herself to with that answer.

CHAPTER 6

"You cook a mean breakfast." Jake smiled as he sipped the steaming coffee from the stoneware mug that Maile had set beside his plate.

They were sitting at the kitchen table. They had made love again, showered together, and then Maile had come out to the kitchen to fix his breakfast.

"Thanks," she murmured self-consciously. "Comes from having had to take care of a house since I was twelve," she added. She started to pick up his empty plate, but he reached out and stopped her.

"Relax. Enjoy your coffee. I'll help with the dishes later."

Maile smiled. "Don't you consider that sort of thing as pure 'woman's work'?" she taunted, her eyes going to his large hands that made the mug look puny.

"No, why should I?" he retorted. "I'm a pretty good cook myself. Comes from living alone." He chuckled at her wide-eyed look. "I see," he whispered. "You thought

I had someone to do things for me." He reached out a hand and lightly caressed her cheek. "I didn't . . . not till now. . . ." He allowed his voice to trail off to a silence pregnant with meaning.

Maile toyed with a fork, making tracks on the white linen spread over the small dinette table, for a moment derisively amused by their small domestic tableau.

"Tell me about you, Maile."

Startled, Maile dropped the fork, snapping irritably, "I thought you already knew everything from Bryan's employment record." He had told her in a moment of complete honesty that he'd had Bryan thoroughly investigated, clear down to finding out where *she* lived, though he had not laid eyes on her until that day at the speedway, and then he had not known that she was Bryan's sister.

"That only told me about Bryan," he returned softly. "I want to know about *you* . . . every little thing about you."

Maile experienced a twinge of unease. Not even Mike— no, not even Bryan, her own flesh and blood—knew the entire workings that blended together to make the Maile Riordan that existed inside the pretty outer packaging. And now *he* wanted to know, and she had a strange suspicion that he would use that knowledge always to hold the upper hand with her.

"What do you want to know?" she asked, both her tone and expression wary.

He smiled; patronizingly, she thought. "Oh, what you like, what you don't like, things like that." He stretched his long legs out, the tips of his toes touching hers.

"That's kind of hard to answer," she replied nervously, being too, too conscious of the seductive rubbing of his foot over hers. "There are so many things I like, and just

107

as many I don't." And at that moment she liked and disliked what he was doing to her, all at once!

"Flowers? Jewelry? Music? Shows? Opera? Food?" The foot continued to move, higher and higher until his toes were teasing the inner part of her thigh.

"Yes. Yes. Yes. Yes. Yes. And yes," she retorted, shivering with the sweetly awful sensations that were shooting up from the thigh being so purposely caressed. Unable to bear the torture any longer, she gathered her legs under her chair, and sat up straighter.

Jake grinned. "I see you're going to be difficult after all." He stood up, lifting her with him. "Come on, let's go do the dishes."

Glad for the reprieve, Maile moved eagerly to the sink and filled the dishpan with hot sudsy water. Plunging the dishes into the dishwater, she forced herself to concentrate on doing them, willing Jake to go to the front room with a beseeching glance thrown his way. But he remained, dish towel in hand, poised and waiting for her to rinse the dishes and give them to him.

After she had shown him where to put the dishes, she hurried into the bedroom to dress.

"Where are we going?" she called out.

"I thought I'd take you back to San Francisco" came the reply from much too close, amused and arrogantly confident. Startled, Maile glanced up and found Jake leaning indolently against the frame of her bedroom door.

"After we take a Red and White tour around the Bay, we can come back to the City, have dinner at the Mark Hopkins and then—" His eyes strayed to the unmade bed, and he grinned. "We can come back here, or you can stay in the City." His grin giving way to a smile that was decidedly wicked, he crossed over to where she was struggling with a zipper that had caught in her black slacks. "Or we don't have to go anywhere at all, honey," he whispered, reaching for her.

"Can't," she replied distractedly, sidestepping to avoid those hard brown hands that would distract her even further. She freed the zipper and ran it up, fastening the one button at her waist almost in the same movement.

Dreading the reaction she would get from him, she lifted her face, smiling as she told him why she could not go with him. "It can't be helped, Jake. I . . . didn't know you'd be here, so I promised to meet with Mike's friends at the track."

He drew a ragged breath. "Ah, yes. Mike's speedway." The derision in his tone made her glance up sharply. His long black lashes briefly veiled the expression in his eyes, and Maile told herself she was seeing things that weren't there. She did not have the power to hurt this man. The truth of this hit her like a physical blow when she met his eyes again, because his eyes were glazed with contempt for her. "Stupid of me, I'd forgotten that you were a career woman—and someone else's."

Bewildered, she frowned, unable to comprehend part of his statement. "I—" *What am I doing? Explaining?* She forced a laugh. "You could change your plans and come with me," she ventured in a pseudocareless tone.

"You know I hate that place," he remarked in a rather bored tone. "Besides, I seem to recall your telling me I had no say in the running of it."

Her cheeks flushed with the recollection. She remembered telling him, too, that she was very particular who her friends were. She smiled self-mockingly. She had just made a liar of herself. Or had she? After all, *lovers* weren't necessarily *friends.*

"Well, you see how it is." She attempted a casual tone, moving to the mirror to do her hair. Her hands trembled as she twirled her hair into a chignon at the top of her head.

"Leave it loose, Maile," crooned that confusing man as he came to stand beside her, his hands reaching out to grab the pins from out of her hand. "Makes you look more feminine . . . deceptively soft," he murmured as his fingers untwirled the heavy coil then raked through the thick mass until her hair was lying softly across her shoulders.

Meeting his eyes in the mirror, Maile had the uncomfortable feeling that he did not think the subject was tabled. He meant to turn her *can't* into *oh, how delightful* or words to that effect.

"Is there no one who—" he started, only to have his words interrupted by the ringing of the phone. "You want me to get that?" he asked grimly. "Or might you be embarrassed?"

Forcing a nervous little laugh, she said, "Now, why would I be embarrassed? After all, you're not the first man to answer my phone," she added lightly, and immediately regretted her words. She had been thinking of Bryan, whose house this had been, and Jake—if she could tell by the strange expression that was flitting across his hardened features—was thinking she was referring to other men.

"Jake, I didn't mean—" She stopped abruptly. Jake was no longer in the room to hear her explanation.

"Who was it?" she asked, trying to keep her interest at a minimum. Unconsciously she crossed her fingers, hoping he would not say it was a wrong number.

"No one," he mumbled, and she cringed. A small shrug seemed to relax the set of his shoulders. "Another case of 'if a man answers. . . .'" His bland expression gave her no clue to his thoughts, but his clenched fists spoke volumes.

"Jake, I—" She was interrupted by the telephone. Jake, who had started to cross the room to the bed, hesitated momentarily, then continued on his way. Maile frowned, debating whether to answer it or ignore its ringing and try to convince Jake that she was not seeing another man. She was positive that that was what he was thinking.

"You'd better go answer it, Maile, and if it bothers you that I'm here, I'll go outside until you've finished your conversation."

The sardonic tone of his words had the same effect on Maile as if she had just heard nails being scraped against a blackboard. She glanced at him in the mirror, her green eyes glinting mutinously. The sight of him took the fight out of her. He was sitting on the bed, his arms folded negligently across his midriff, his head resting on the headboard. For a moment his expression was unguarded, and she had a glimpse of his inner turmoil. But she would not believe what his reflection told her. No. Jake Weston did not love her, so why would he be jealous?

She spun around on the bench, eager to have a closer look, but it was too late. He had become aware of her scrutiny through the mirror, and now his expression was one of complete indifference.

Sighing ruefully, Maile slid from the vanity bench and went to answer the phone.

"Hello."

"Maile?" David's voice was guarded.

"Yes. Is something wrong, Dave?" Maile frowned when she saw Jake coming toward her. What had happened to his resolve not to eavesdrop? she wondered. A shiver zipped up her spine as Jake lifted one hand to brush long brown fingers across her lips, and she moved away from him.

"I just called to tell you that I won't be seeing you today," came the unhappy reply. "I—" Maile gasped when Jake's hand moved with wicked purpose to the pearl buttons that fastened her blouse. His fingers were cool and competent—from years of experience, she thought sourly, shrugging him off.

"What was that?" Maile almost shouted into the phone. Jake moved around, sending his arms to embrace her waist. Maile turned her head, trapping the phone against her shoulder, leaving both hands free to push Jake away from her.

"Is something wrong, Maile? Your voice sounds funny."

"No!" she hissed at Jake; then, "No, Dave, nothing's wrong. What's with you?" She closed her eyes tightly, trying to shut out the sight of the handsome face so close to hers. Jake chuckled, then his mouth closed bruisingly over hers, and she had to fight against an engulfing sensation in order to hear what David was saying to her.

"Nothing's wrong, Maile, it's just that something's come up suddenly, and I can't come out to the track today."

Maile felt her sanity slipping away as Jake's mouth moved purposely over hers. David's voice in her ear was like a distant humming until he sensed she was not paying attention to him and hollered her name.

Wrenching her mouth from Jake's, Maile breathed huskily into the phone, "You don't have to scream. I'm listening."

"You didn't seem to be" was the sullen rejoinder.

Taking a deep breath, Maile repeated what he had said to her, adding, "So, I guess I'll see you Sunday, then."

"No, Maile, not Sunday, either. My uncle's coming down and wants me to do something with him on Sunday."

Maile quivered with feeling as Jake's hands slipped into her blouse, his fingers shooting tiny electric shocks through her body as they moved around to her back. She withheld a moan that started deep in her chest when he bent his head to kiss the breast he had maneuvered free of her bra and blouse. *Lord, how much more can I stand?*

"Right, Dave, see you later," she managed breathlessly, fervently thankful the boy had decided against prolonging their conversation. Blindly she reached out and dropped the phone onto its cradle.

"Your young friend from the track?" Jake asked, the voice muffled against her breast. Maile nodded against his head pressed so tightly to the valley between her breasts. She closed her eyes, letting her mind go blank as her hungry body enjoyed his caresses, knowing she could no more fight him off than she could stop the sun from shining.

A moment later she was standing alone by the phone, her breath coming in ragged gulps. Jake was way across the room, toying with one of Mike's racing trophies. She blinked. What had she done *now*?

A pulse throbbed wildly at his temple as his narrowed eyes lingered on the engraved name. MICHAEL SLOAN. He shivered inwardly at the savagery of the emotions that were aroused by the realization that the woman he wanted was still in love with another man. No, strike that. With the *memory* of another man: with his ghost. Biting down hard on his back teeth, Jake managed to restrain himself from destroying all the trophies, all the pictures and posters that stood between them like a physical barrier.

"Did he cancel out on you?" he asked without turning around.

"Who?"

"Your friend from the track."

"Yes. But that doesn't change anything, Jake," Maile added quietly when she saw his broad shoulders relax. "I wasn't going out there just to meet David. My date is with Mike's friends, who are going to outline what needs to be done before we can open the speedway." She cleared her throat nervously and waited for him to say something.

Jake inclined his head mockingly, and finally set down Mike's trophy with exaggerated care. When he turned to her, Maile was stunned to see a hard, unpleasant look in his eyes.

"I suppose I'd best be on my way," he muttered.

"Will you come back later?" she asked, stiffening her backbone with Irish pride to keep from running to him to beg him to stay.

"Probably not." He offered no explanation, and she was afraid to say anything else for fear she would start bawling like a baby.

Trembling fingers somehow managed to refasten the buttons he had undone, her attention riveted to her fingers to keep him from seeing the wet pain his refusal to come back had put in her eyes.

"I have to get to the speedway," she mumbled, pushing the last button through its buttonhole. She swallowed past the lump in her throat, praying fervently that she would not give him a hint of the misery gnawing at her insides as she went past him.

Hurt put an emerald glow in her eyes, yet pride kept her

114

from putting her pain into words, from crying out, "Why can't you love me the way I love you?" Woodenly she moved across the room, picked up her purse and slung it across her shoulder. Pride was her mainstay: it gave her control of turbulent emotions, and she managed to move past Jake at the door with a nonchalance she did not feel.

She stood by the door, waiting for him to step out in front of her. "I haven't all day," she said stiltedly when she saw Jake hesitate.

He looked down at her for long seconds, his eyes filled with a warm expression, but she returned his gaze steadily, unemotionally. Slowly he reached out, took her purse from her, and dropped it on the floor.

"We are not going to part like this," he whispered as his arm slid around her, drawing her to him. "You seem angry with me. Why?" The thinness of her silk blouse could not ward off the scorching fire of his touch; nor could her reeling senses quell the desire to be held even closer to him. Maile closed her eyes against the intense longing that was rippling through her. Catching back the crazy urge to put her desire into words, to beg him to love her, she whispered hoarsely, "Please, Jake, don't. Let me go, I'm late."

"Don't what?" he teased, bending his head down to hers, with slow deliberation beginning to kiss the stiffness from her face, creating a tide of rising passion that she seemed unable to control.

"Don't do that!" she gasped, wrenching her mouth from his as his hands began to fondle her intimately. Her green eyes looked up at him luminously, betraying the passion he had aroused in her. "Let me go, Jake!"

"And what if I don't want to?" he asked softly, hugging her struggling body to him. "I think I'll just take you back to your bedroom and keep you there the entire day and night, making love to you over and over again—until I can cool down the fire you light in me."

Maile's cheeks went pink. Suddenly she knew what his game was: He was trying to keep her from meeting Mike's friends at the speedway. She tried to twist free, but his hold was too strong. Angry now, she placed her hands flat on his chest and pushed with all her might.

"I have obligations, Jake!" she cried as her very last effort failed.

"Your first obligation is to me, the man you love," he pointed out arrogantly.

"Oh?" She felt the flash of angry color touch her skin. He had some nerve, reminding her that she loved him when no words of love had yet crossed his lips! She breathed in deeply, trying to keep a rein on her rising temper.

"Uh-huh." He pressed soft kisses along her neck and jaw, his hands taking bold license with her body, molding her against him to make her aware of his growing virility.

She made a feeble attempt to resist him only to have his arms tighten around her until she was gasping for breath. His mouth covered hers hungrily, claiming possession, brooking no resistance, moving from her mouth only of its own volition, and then only to trail light nibbling kisses to her chin, across the length of her neck, and on down to the soft quivering mound of flesh cupped in his hand. His tongue snaked out, and with maddening slowness, it lightly teased the nipple into trembling erection through the flimsy garment that covered it.

Her body arched against him of its own will; she was on fire from his caresses. Impatient with the slow movements of his mouth, her hands went up, her fingers grasping his hair, holding his head down while she merged her mouth with his.

Perversely he pulled back, trailing his mouth across her cheek. "Tell me now that you wouldn't rather stay with me," he taunted softly, lifting his eyes to look into hers. He dropped a tantalizingly slow kiss on her warm mouth, and teased, "Tell me how you'd much rather go watch the little boys play than stay here and do your own playing . . . with a man."

You cad! You miserable wicked fiend! she cried in her mind. Desperately she tried to break free, twisting and pushing against him until one large hand came up to twine itself in the thickness of her hair and she could no longer move to escape the sensuous torment of his lips, searching, probing, arrogantly demanding a response.

When he finally decided to release her, Maile was gasping for breath, and her lips had that lightly swollen look of someone who has been thoroughly and ruthlessly kissed. Aroused passion had put a deep, dark emerald glow in her eyes and a healthy, becoming blush on her cheeks.

He was grinning, and his eyes expressed the triumph he was feeling: knowing that he could master her with sensual pleasure had put a wicked gleam in his blue eyes.

"Well, now," he mocked sweetly, "guess we both know that, given the right circumstances, we would lock ourselves away in your bedroom, wouldn't we?"

Maile could not bear to see his proud expression, and looked away in embarrassed silence.

"Wouldn't we?" His voice no longer held a mocking tone; it was obnoxiously sober.

"No," she whispered almost inaudibly, refusing to admit to him that he was right.

"Shall I convince you some more?" His voice was cool; the expression in his eyes determined, as though he meant to have complete victory over her—as though he would not settle for anything less than her total submission.

"No!" Her voice cracked, and she cleared her throat nervously, inching away. "No, that won't be necessary." She edged farther away, willing strength into her shaky legs. She looked longingly at Mike's chair, wishing she could just sit down for a few minutes, but she knew she dared not remain in the house with Jake.

"And here I was looking forward to it," he teased as she took the first step toward the door.

I'll just bet you were! As she bent down to pick up her purse from the floor, she felt his blue eyes burning into her back. Turning as she straightened, she caught those piercing eyes gliding over her, possessive pleasure gleaming in their blue depths.

That's it, she thought, her breath catching in her throat. *He wants to own me, to maneuver me around like a mindless puppet.* And she knew that if she stayed with him today, her defeat would be easy and complete.

Nervously Maile slung her purse over her shoulder and opened the door. But Jake did not move through it. She stared at him in confusion, wondering what was holding him back this time. Certainly he would not resort to pulling such a childish trick as stalling to keep her from going to meet with Mike's friends.

This is ridiculous, she thought, shifting position against the door while Jake stood where she had left him, looking at her with an inscrutable expression on his face.

"Well, are you going?" she snapped.

"Yes." He smiled. "But I'm coming back to take you to dinner." His smile widening, he teased, "It's not just

118

women who reserve the right to change their minds, you know."

Maile shrugged with impatience. He was out to drive her nuts; she just knew it. That's why he kept changing his mind.

"You shouldn't think bad thoughts of me," he chided, smiling as he crossed over to where she stood waiting at the door. "Your expressions give them all away." Chuckling deep in his throat, he cupped her chin and lifted her face to his. Slowly he bent down and very gently brushed his lips across hers.

"I am coming back, Maile," he promised. "And if you don't mind, I'd like to stay." Maile gasped, and while he had her at a disadvantage, he added, "And I think I'll bring my toothbrush and razor with me this time." Giving her no time to gather her scattered wits enough to make any kind of reply, he went out of the house, whistling softly, happily, leaving Maile to stare after him, her lips still tingling with his kiss, her mind troubled.

"Damn, damn, damn!" she muttered under her breath as she went out, slamming the door behind her for good measure. "I think I'll bring my toothbrush and razor!" she mocked harshly.

As she slid in behind the wheel of her car, she felt her own practical sanity returning, and she knew, without a doubt, that come Sunday morning, she was *not* going to find his razor, his toothbrush, or anything else of his on the mirrored shelf in her bathroom! At least, she amended with a growing smile, until he was willing to make a commitment.

As she drove through the gate a few minutes later, she recalled what Jake had said and smiled. First, he had told her that he didn't think he was coming to see her, and then he had done a volte-face and told her he was staying with her!

"My, my, my!" she whispered, grinning, feeling a trifle smug about his change of mind.

In the next two hours, as Mike's friends put her through the ropes up in the observation tower where the announcer sat during the races, she forgot about Jake almost completely.

George Mason, a small wiry man with a penchant for "getting things done yesterday" left no doubt that he knew what he was doing. As Maile's manager, he moved around the track with a pad and pencil, jotting down things he told Maile she should get repaired, or changed, before she reopened the speedway. Maile trailed after him like a child trying to keep up with an adult who was taking two long strides to her every one. She felt breathless, but she didn't know whether it was because she was finally moving toward the grand opening, or because she was having a hard time keeping step with him.

Dean Reynolds, Mike's top mechanic, joined them briefly to tell Maile that he had talked to all of Mike's sponsors, and every one of them had agreed to work with her. Maile was deeply grateful, and embarrassed the man by throwing her arms around him and kissing him.

His ruddy complexion went redder still. "You know, Maile, that sort of thing's bound to get you in trouble with some of the others," he cautioned. "Now, me, I know you don't mean nothing by it, but—" He threw a glance at George, shrugged, and moved away.

Maile managed not to laugh, and assured him that she would try to keep her hands to herself in the future, clasping them in front of her as she resumed her walk.

Mickey Green—part-time teacher, part-time racer, and full-time fan of Mike's—interrupted her to tell her she had a phone call back at the tower.

Thinking it was Jake calling her to cancel their date, Maile moved slowly toward the tower, taxing her brain to come up with something that would force him to come back.

But it was Janey calling from the boutique.

"Lord, I'm glad I caught you there, Maile. Verna Johnson's down here—"

"On a Saturday?" Maile interrupted, a twinge of irritation showing in her tone. "And what were you doing down there? I thought you needed a break."

"I only came in to pick up a remnant to make my little niece a doll's dress . . . and there was Verna, pacing up and down in front of the door. I tried to tell her that we weren't open, but she insisted that I let her in, and then she *demanded* that I call you and get you over here." Her voice dropped until it was hard for Maile to hear her, what with the fellows discussing plans right behind her. "She brought in her own portfolio, and you wouldn't believe what she wants us to do!"

"Give me about twenty—no, thirty minutes, Janey."

"Can't you make it any sooner? She's in a terrible snit."

"If she can't wait, Janey, she can come back," Maile said firmly, her tone warning Janey that she did not wish to argue on the phone.

"Well, all right," Janey capitulated ungraciously. "But don't be late. I don't want to have to put up with her longer than I have to." And she let the receiver drop noisily to its cradle.

Maile's thoughts exploded. How dare that woman be so—so overbearing and bossy! Clenching her hands, she

121

turned to the men behind her, urging them to continue with what they had been trying to teach her. But her mind was on the woman waiting for her in the shop, and little or nothing they said made sense. Sensing that she was preoccupied, they promised they would stay and get things ready, and she could go do whatever she needed to do at the boutique.

"You guys are great," she said, her voice bubbling with sincerity. It was true—they were great, and she was beginning to see them as individuals, and liking them more now that they didn't seem like obstacles between her and Mike.

Mike! She was able to smile, thinking of him as she left the tower and went down to her car. Mike would have been in hysterics seeing her trying to assimilate what his friends were trying to teach her.

"Ah, Mike!" she breathed, sliding in behind the wheel. He would always have a small corner of her heart; but now she could think of him, remember how much she had loved him without her entire heart shriveling with pain. And it was all thanks to Jake, she thought in a moment of complete self-honesty.

CHAPTER 7

"Lord, I thought you'd never get here!" Janey hissed as Maile came into the workroom. Janey accused in a hoarse whisper that Maile was a coward because she had ducked into the shop through the back door, effectively avoiding Mrs. Johnson, who was waiting like a predator in the showroom.

"I parked in the back," Maile said, defending herself and grinning as she dropped her purse on the worktable. Drawing herself up, she pushed through the door, then smiled and made her presence known to the woman pacing up and down in front of the sales counter.

"Mrs. Johnson, what a surprise!" she exclaimed in a voice she hoped did not show even a slight twinge of the irritation she still felt. Feeling like a hypocrite while doing it, she enlarged her smile and held out her hand.

The older woman was definitely upset about something. Her lips trembled as she smiled, and it took her a few moments to realize Maile's hand was still stretched out to her.

Clasping her hand, Verna Johnson drew Maile toward her and in a threateningly tearful whisper, explained that her husband had ordered her to have a new gown made to *his* specifications. Maile looked up, startled. Was *that* any reason to cry? Although she did not like anyone making demands like that on her, she found it sweet of Mr. Johnson to care so much for his wife, and voiced her opinion.

"Sweet!" screamed the distraught wife. "He said I needed something that would make me look—" She choked off the rest of the words, leaving Maile impatient to know what Mr. Johnson could have said to put his wife in such a state.

Chic? Appealing? Sexy? The words followed each other through Maile's mind as she ran her eyes over the woman's tall, slender form. With that naturally blond hair, model's form, beguiling blue eyes, and a sensual husky voice—what more could her husband want? Maile thought a trifle irritably.

Eyes tearing, Verna Johnson admitted that her husband had drawn up a few designs that he thought would make her look *younger.* Maile foresaw a migraine the moment the woman brought out an architect's portfolio, and she was right. By the time she had studied the six designs Mr. Johnson had drawn, she had a doozy of a headache.

"Leave them with us, Mrs. Johnson. Janey and I will go over them, and see what we can come up with." Praying silently for a fire that would destroy the Johnson designs even if her entire shop went with them, Maile took the sketches and laid them on the counter. Trying not to physically push the woman out of the shop, she urged her out, only half listening to her chatter.

"I'll see you in two weeks, then?" Verna Johnson smiled, relieved, it seemed, to leave everything in Maile's capable hands.

"Yes. By that time Janey and I will have something for you that your husband cannot help but like," Maile assured her with more confidence than she felt.

"Oh, I knew I could count on you, Maile," the woman gushed, a smile stretching wide the carefully painted lips.

"You handled that like a pro," teased Janey as Maile came back into the shop.

Maile swirled around and demanded, "Where were you when I needed you?"

Janey grinned, her dark eyes twinkling. "Outside with the cutest hunk of man I've ever seen." She laughed; then, turning, she called out, "All right, it's safe to come in." Almost before her words were out David came strolling into the showroom, grinning.

"Why didn't you tell me you had Janey Apella working for you?" he asked, moving toward Maile with a mock-furious expression on his face.

Wide-eyed, Maile looked from David to Janey and back again. "I didn't know you two knew each other," she said, and the two younger people laughed.

"We don't," David admitted, his grin lighting up his eyes. "At least we didn't. . . ."

Again his grin was reminiscent of someone else's but Maile could not remember whose. Nor did she have the time to speculate on it, she reminded herself, for two weeks wasn't near enough time to come up with a design for Mrs. Johnson that her husband would consider youthful, appealing, sexy, becoming *and* not outrageously priced.

"Can't be done," predicted Janey gloomily.

"Are you going to be working all day?" David interjected while Maile thought of something to say that would take that mulish look from Janey's face.

"Why are you here anyway?" she asked, belatedly wondering why he was here at the shop when he had told her he was going to be too occupied to even go to the track.

He shrugged. "Things fell through," he told her with a tone of dismissal, but Maile wouldn't accept that. Finally, out of sheer desperation, he told her that he had had a date with his uncle, who had called at the last minute to cancel. "He's probably too busy with some chick, if I know my uncle."

He grinned. "You should meet him—no, it's probably best that you don't. You girls are much too pretty, and much too innocent." He chuckled. "You know the old saying, An apple a day . . . ? Well, my uncle has changed it to: A woman a day . . ." Again that mocking chuckle that nagged at Maile's memory.

"It's past lunchtime, so how about going out with me— the two of you?" His eyes twinkled as they went to Janey's eager expression.

"You two go on," Maile suggested sweetly. "I think I'd best get started on that design." As she was talking she was walking to the workroom, sketchpad under her arm.

"Are you sure you don't want to join us?" Janey asked —in such a negative tone that it made Maile chuckle as she complied with her unspoken request and refused to join them.

Giving a rueful grin, she sat down at her desk under the window and went to work, wondering why, *now*, Mr.

Johnson was pestering his wife about her age. Though nearly forty, Verna was fortunate enough to look no older than a chic thirty. She shook her head. It seemed, she told herself with a sigh, that some men just couldn't be satisfied with what they already had.

Hours later her sketchpad was still blank, her mind in the same condition. She sighed with exasperation, hunching her shoulders to ease the nagging ache that was burning between her shoulder blades. This was as bad as sitting in front of a typewriter all day, she thought, slapping the sketchpad down on the desk. She stood up, rotating her head to ease the tension that had stiffened her shoulders.

If she had used half the sense the good Lord had given her, she could've seen immediately that this task was one she should shy away from. But, no, her greed had gotten the best of her, and here she was—working on a Saturday when she should be out at the speedway.

The ringing of the telephone interrupted her thoughts and, muttering to herself, she went to answer it, wondering what other catastrophe could possibly befall her today.

"Hi, lover."

"Jake." The tension slipped away from her shoulders, and she smiled.

"I thought you were going to spend the day at the track?"

"I meant to, Jake, but then something happened here at the shop, and I had to come here." She knew she sounded a little impatient, but it was too late to change her tone.

"Something's wrong," he said.

"No, Jake, nothing's wrong. At least nothing that can't be taken care of," she lied, wrinkling her nose in annoyance as she recalled the obnoxiously empty sketchpad on her desk.

"That's my girl, always thinking positive." He laughed. "Look, my plans kind of fell through, so why don't you come back home and have lunch with me . . . or an early dinner . . . or—" He laughed again, a rich seductive sound that tickled her senses, and made her smile.

"*Lunch* sounds divine. I'm hungry."

"Then, come on home, baby. . . ."

Maile heard the click on the phone before it sank into her brain that Jake had been calling from her house. But how . . . ? *How?* She *knew* how: with her extra key. She shook her head incredulously. He had never taken advantage of that key before, so why now?

Because he was making himself at home. It both annoyed and pleased her, but the negative reaction was by far the stronger. Realizing that she still held the phone to her ear, she dropped it, and went into the workroom for her purse. She locked the back door, then went through the shop, turning off all the lights before going out and locking the door behind her.

Thirty minutes later she drove into her driveway, but she did not immediately get out of her car. She sat with her arms crossed over the steering wheel, looking up at her house, wondering why she felt such a strong hesitation to go in.

Unreasonably, or so she tried to convince herself, her temper started to rise. She slammed out of the car and dashed up the walk to her house. By the time she had reached the door, she found a reason for her ill mood. Jake was just too pushy. And he had taken away from her the option of inviting him into her house or telling him to go take a flying leap!

Anger put a lovely blush on her skin, and it was the first thing that Jake noticed as she breezed into the house.

The man really has a knack for doing and saying the wrong things, she fumed as Jake moved toward her, whispering that he knew what had put that heightened color on her face.

"It's a glow that always gives a woman away when she's been with a man," he teased audaciously, reaching out to take her in his arms.

"Is that what you really believe?" she snapped, green eyes smoldering as she sidestepped to avoid his arms.

He grinned—a little too confidently, she thought, feeling a painful throbbing beginning at her temples. "It's what I *know,* sweetheart," he cooed. "That glow would tell the whole world that you are a completely satisfied woman."

Maile was too angry to be embarrassed by what he was implying. "Then the whole damn world would be wrong," she said irritably. She flung her purse across the room, landing it unerringly on the couch. The only time that she had perfect aim was when she was almost blind with anger. "This 'glow' that you're crowing about comes from anger, Jake, and *that* comes from finding out that you've invaded my home."

Jake's dark head snapped back as though she had slapped him. His smile vanished with lightning swiftness, and an austere, rather gray cast appeared on his face. His eyes grew hard and cold as they centered on her flushed face; they narrowed fiercely.

"I apologize," he said, the words drawn through his clenched teeth. "I thought, after what we've shared, that I was a little more than a *casual* acquaintance. I guess I was mistaken." Picking his coat off the back of the couch, he went past her to the door.

"In case you're interested, Maile, I did not *invade* your

home . . . nor would I." He was by the door by this time, his coat slung across his shoulder, one foot already on the porch. "Your next-door neighbor saw me waiting in the car and came across to ask me what I was doing. When I told her, she offered to let me in. She insisted it was what you would want her to do." He smiled, but it was not a pretty smile. "I guess the lady doesn't know you any better than I do." He went out, closing the door very quietly behind him. The very softness of his action seemed to reverberate through the suddenly deathlike stillness of the house.

"Oh, Jake, I'm sorry—"

But it was too late. She heard the sound of his car starting and by the time she had run to the door, and then out to the porch, he was already gone from her driveway.

She could not stay in the house. After eating a Spartan lunch, she changed into jeans and an old sweat shirt of Mike's that was still in her closet and went back to the speedway.

Hands clasped behind her, Maile walked around the empty track, recalling the first day she had seen Jake. She had been there to exorcise Mike's ghost, never dreaming that a man of such imposing personality as Jake would show up and within a few weeks become the most important person in her life.

She heard a car coming and, turning, she saw Jake's red Ferrari coming through the gate. She froze where she was, almost not daring to breathe. Had he come here to make up? Or was it something else? She couldn't tell by his expression, and she steeled herself for the worst.

"I thought this was where I'd find you."

"Jake, I—"

"No, Maile. For once in your life, just listen—I've come to apologize."

"Me, too, Jake," she said, smiling tentatively.

"Shhh." He covered the distance between them and stood looking down at her without even attempting to touch her.

"I rode around for a bit, wondering what had gotten into you to turn you into such a shrew. And then it hit me. Inadvertently I *had* invaded your home. You were right to be angry." Very slowly, as though he were afraid to touch her for fear of being rejected, he lifted his hands to her arms, and then drew her gently to him. Looking deep into her eyes, he grinned. "I'm running up the white flag, Maile."

"There's no need to," she said, lifting her face for his kiss.

He smiled, his sober look disappearing. "I think, honey, that I'm the one to judge whether there's a need for it or not."

She smiled under his lips. Arrogant as always, but oh, how she loved him. And if she had lost him over such a petty little thing, she would have hated herself for the rest of her days.

"Where are you going?" he demanded as she freed herself and started to move toward her car.

"Home, Jake. Come on." Without turning back to see if he was following, she hurried to her car and climbed in.

Shaking his head, Jake came to her window and made her roll it down. "Are we cooking dinner at home or eating out?"

She quivered as his hand went into the car to stroke her cheek. Then she was leaning against that hand, rubbing it with her cheek as it rested on her shoulder.

131

"What do you want to fix?" he asked softly, leaning his elbow on the door, ducking his head inside the window to kiss her. "I'll stop at the store and get whatever you want."

"Oh, you're being too congenial," she accused with a laugh, pushing him away. "But all right. I'll fix dinner at home. I guess you're tired of eating out all the time.

"Get whatever you want, but don't get too carried away. I don't intend to spend all night in the kitchen."

"I wouldn't want you to," he murmured. Then he lifted his head out of the car and, rapping his knuckles on the roof, turned and went to his own car, his steps firm, unhurried.

Maile watched him drive out of the gate without stopping. So he's going to let me do the locking up this time, she thought amusedly as she started her car. She drove out slowly, stopped, and left the car to go and lock the gate.

With a sigh of weariness she climbed back in her car, sitting without moving for a few minutes, rehashing the events of the day. It was no wonder she was suddenly so tired, she thought, throwing her car into gear. Men! She smiled, unable to summon the energy to get angry at the men who had caused such turmoil in her day—Mr. Johnson and Jake. She slid one slim hand under the heavy fall of blue-black hair to rub the back of her neck, rotating her head to ease the weariness that had put a tickling ache between her shoulder blades.

Jake's car was parked in her driveway, and with a smile Maile opened her car door and got out.

"I was going to say I was surprised to find you here already, but knowing the way you drive . . . ." Grinning mischievously, she reached out and opened his car door. "Or did you even stop at the store?" she added after she had peeked into his car and seen nothing that even vaguely resembled a bag of groceries.

"You decided not to brave my cooking, eh?" She stepped back as he slung his long legs out from the car and stood up.

"I thought I'd take you out, Maile," he said, draping an arm around her as they started toward the porch. "How does the Cliff House strike you? Or Plateau Seven? Or the Acapulco?"

Maile laughed softly. Every restaurant he mentioned took him verbally closer to San Francisco, and his home.

"Surprise me," she said as she scrounged through her bag for her key. Although what she anticipated he would say would come as no surprise.

And it didn't. Taking the key from her hand, he unlocked the door and pushed it open. With a large hand lightly pressing the small of her waist, he urged her into the house and followed her in before he spoke. "How about coming home with me? I want to show you that I wasn't just bragging when I told you I knew how to cook."

"I've got a better idea," Maile said. "Why don't you just show me how well you can cook right here?" She dropped her purse on a nearby table and turned to face him. And she found him frowning, his gaze fixed on Mike's picture across the room.

"What?" He blinked. The smile that curved his mouth did not quite reach to his eyes. They were cold and hard.

Maile did not answer. Her eyes went to Mike's smiling face, her mind on the day he had given her that picture. "It was just sitting in a drawer, feeling lonesome," Mike had told her, and even now she could see that funny little smile that had curved his mouth when he had asked her if she wanted it. *I'm not ready to give you up completely,*

Mike, she told the silent face, and yet . . . there stood Jake: tall, handsome, vibrantly alive, but unhappy because everywhere he looked, he saw something that reminded him of Mike.

Biting the corner of her lower lip, Maile stood undecided for a moment, then turned her face up to look at Jake again.

"Go get ready, Maile, I'm starved." His voice was toneless.

"Make yourself a drink," she invited quietly, indicating the teak cabinet standing in the corner of the room. "I am going to be a little while. . . ." Her voice trailed behind her as she slipped past him and hurried into her room. Feeling her pulses quicken when her gaze fell on the rumpled bed, she forced herself to move into the bathroom, and turned on only the cold water in the shower.

Gooseflesh rose quickly on her arms and then all over her body when she stepped under the pelting rain of the shower, but it was just what she needed to banish the sensual thoughts that the rumpled bed had brought to the surface in her mind.

"I thought you'd like to have your back scrubbed," murmured a husky voice while a large bronzed hand tickled her back with its feather-soft, unexpected caress. Maile screamed, startled as well as annoyed. But before she could chide him for being so pushy, Jake's other hand reached over her shoulder and turned on the hot-water faucet. "You little idiot! What the hell are you trying to do, catch pneumonia?" he bellowed, pulling her out of the shower and immediately wrapping her in his warm embrace.

"Jake, let me go!" she cried, pushing forward to release herself. But instead of letting her go, he held her closer.

134

After a moment he reached his hand into the shower again, felt the water, and then told her she could go back in and finish.

Her shaky legs would not hold her up when Jake released her, but his arm kept her from folding. He laughed. "Why don't you forget the shower and get dressed?" He didn't give her a chance to reply. Bending swiftly, he lifted her in his arms and carried her into the bedroom.

"Get dressed," he ordered, laughing as he dumped her in the middle of the bed.

"You miserable fiend!" she whispered furiously as the water bed rocked beneath her. He had known why she was taking that cold shower, and also why her knees had buckled under her when he let go. And he was proud of it, if she could tell by the sound of the low, masculine laughter that trailed behind him as he left her bedroom.

Rolling off the bed dried her body, yet she went back into the bathroom, turned off the shower, grabbed a towel off the rack, and briskly rubbed her body until every inch of her tingled. Slipping on a long black slip, she crossed over to the closet and stood there for a moment, wondering what to wear. Wanting to look chic, she started for one of her own creations, a long turquoise crepe that fastened behind the neck, leaving her shoulders and back deliciously bare. But then she changed her mind and pulled out a black silk skirt and white tricot blouse with cowl neck. Pleased with the effect this combination gave her, she sat at her vanity and begin to comb her hair. Remembering that Jake liked it down, she smiled with sensual delight and coiled it in a bun at her nape, telling herself that it would be more fun for Jake to loosen it himself. Lightly shading her upper lids with a teal-blue shadow, she then applied colorless lip gloss to her lips and pronounced herself ready to go out.

Jake's low wolf whistle was all any girl could want for approval, but he added to it by suggesting that they lock the front door, take the phone off the hook, and pretend they were photographers.

"Photographers?" Maile repeated, giving him a look that eloquently expressed her doubt for his sanity.

"Sure." He grinned. "Then we could just wait to see what develops. . . ." He chuckled at her reaction, then told her to get her coat.

"Hmm. I thought you wanted to stay here and see what developed," she teased over her shoulder as she went back to her bedroom to get her coat.

A ripple of arrogant male laughter followed her into the room, and then the rest of Jake Weston followed. "Whatever gave you the idea the same thing won't happen to you in my home that happened here?" His deep, husky voice did strange things to her nervous system and, coupled with his words, it sent a shiver up Maile's spine. Knowing she was outclassed, she found it infinitely wiser to keep her mouth shut.

Grabbing her leather coat from the closet, she preceded Jake out of her room and out of the house. As he reached out to open her door Maile turned and found him looking at her, a strange expression in his eyes that she found unpleasantly disturbing.

"Something wrong, Jake?" she asked quietly, her eyes focused on the large hand on the car door, the knuckles looking unnaturally pale against the red of the paint.

He mumbled something under his breath, and then he grasped her shoulders and pulled her roughly against him, lifting her completely off the ground.

"Jake, what's the matter with you?" she shrieked, her voice catching on a laugh. "Put me down, for goodness' sake! What'll the neighbors think?" she demanded, looking over her shoulder, thinking that Janice at least would be looking out the window with a censuring—if not envying—eye.

Jake groaned and then muttered, "They'll think I'm crazy," as he brought his mouth down hard on hers. They won't be the only ones! Maile thought before all conscious thought left her as her body began to respond to the hungry male body against which she was pressed so passionately.

"You're a witch, Maile Riordan," he accused in a soft, throaty murmur that made her tingle to her toes with pleasure. "You've bewitched me until I can't think of anything but making love to you." Then his mouth began plundering hers almost harshly, demanding entrance into the sweet, moist inner cavern, dissatisfied until Maile surrendered to him completely.

Maile felt the world slowly slipping away; the early evening sounds faded to a dull murmur in her ears as she was pulled into a whirlpool of intense, electrifying pleasure. Fire licked at her limbs, trickling quicksilver through her veins. A familiar weakening of her legs made her send her arms around his neck, whereas before they had been lightly wrapped around his waist.

"Ah, Mike," she breathed.

Mike! That soft whisper should have carried Jake's name, not another's! Jake felt a knife thrust of jealousy pierce his heart, and he groaned.

Maile heard his groan, and then she was suddenly coldly thrust away. Unaware of what she had done, she bit down on her lower lip in confusion. "What now?" she demanded, her passion-glazed eyes lifted to meet the wintry gaze bent to her.

A muscle started throbbing wildly at his jaw. His mouth moved, but no words were forthcoming. Feeling her own sanity slipping away, Maile gripped the top of the door for equilibrium as his eyes narrowed with the hard, cold look that was becoming much too familiar.

"You know, you're a very difficult man to understand, Jake Weston," she said, attempting to inject a little levity into the strained atmosphere that bristled between them.

"Oh, so you do know my name," he jeered through clenched teeth.

Startled, Maile blinked and then shook her head, wondering what *that* had to do with anything. Eyes narrowed in confusion skimmed over his grim features, but they found no clue to his thoughts.

"I really don't know what you're talking about, Jake," she said quietly. "You're not making much sense."

"You really don't know?" he countered, an incredulous ring in his tone. Maile shook her head, her eyes beseeching him to enlighten her. But he was stubbornly mute. And she, unfortunately, could not read his mind.

Unable to cope with the strained silence growing between them, Maile fidgeted uncomfortably and finally decided it was no use standing there with his moodiness hanging over her like a black cloud. She went around him, then forced herself to walk calmly to the porch.

"Come back here, Maile." His command cut like a whip through the air, its impact sending a shiver through her body.

"Whatever for, Jake?" Maile demanded, her tone more weary than frightened. She quickened her step, climbed up to the porch, then went to sit on the swing. She rested her

138

head against the slatted back of the swing and closed her eyes, allowing her troubled thoughts free rein.

His words echoed eerily in her mind again and again: "Oh, so you do know my name." But no matter how many times she thought them over, she could not understand why he had made such a disquieting statement.

And he's not going to tell me, she thought, cracking open one eye and finding Jake still standing beside his car, his expression unchanged.

Sighing, she left the swing and started back into the house, only to be halted by Jake's voice.

"Maile, wait."

Slowly, she turned around, her eyes glazed with hope. "What is it, Jake?"

His answer, when it finally came, surprised her as much as his earlier rejection had. "I'm hungry. How about you?" He gave her a smile reminiscent of his characteristic one, but it was miles short of being happy.

Maile stared at him, her eyes fully expressing her total confusion. Then, shrugging, she went back to him.

"Since you're all decked out to go to a fancy restaurant and I'm not, I think I'll go home first to bathe and change. And then you can have your pick of restaurants in the City." Helping her into the car, he then closed the door gently behind her and went around to the driver's side. As he slid in behind the wheel he expelled his breath in a sigh that seemed to fill the entire car.

Maile shivered with a strange, unshakable sense of doom. Something had changed between them and, somehow, judging by the whitened knuckles gripping the wheel, whatever it was would end up being her fault. This was a proud, haughty man she was dealing with. How could she expect him to share blame, or heap it solely upon

139

his own broad shoulders? She lifted her eyes to his face—and what a face! Even the presidential countenances carved on Mount Rushmore had nothing on that physiognomy!

"You're not very happy with me, Jake," she ventured with forced bravado.

"What makes you think that?"

"Oh, didn't you know? I'm a mind reader," she returned, her tone slightly flippant.

"Then, tell me what I'm thinking now," he muttered, and before she could guess what he was about, he leaned forward and grabbed her in his arms.

"I'm *Jake*," he said against her lips. "J-A-K-E!"

"Yes, Jake," she whispered meekly as his mouth settled masterfully over hers.

"Now, let's go eat," he said, straightening himself with a shrug.

If I live to be a hundred, Jake Weston, I'm sure I'll never understand your swift changes of mood, she told him silently, her sweet smile successfully hiding the irritation bubbling in her breast.

CHAPTER 8

An essential part of any driver's race-car effort is his pit crew. For David this consisted of four girls: one brunette, one redhead, and two blondes. Maile watched him driving in, followed by the girls in a bright green dune buggy. She smiled. David's private cheering section. The girls were in uniform: tight, flared-leg designer jeans and a green T-shirt with a broad yellow stripe across each well-formed chest.

No sooner had David parked his car than he was running up to the tower.

"Cute pit crew you got there," Maile teased as he came in.

He grinned, then sobered. "Don't let their appearances fool you, Maile. Those four could strip a car in record time, and keep all their nails intact."

"Ah! But stripping it is one thing, Dave, and changing a tire and—"

"Oh, they know what they're doing." He looked down

to where the girls were waiting for him by his car and grinned. "At any rate I didn't come up here to talk about the girls. I came to thank you for getting Boyden off my back."

"You're welcome."

He smiled sheepishly. "But he's got something else on me, Maile." He drew an envelope out of the breast pocket of his coveralls, and silently held it out to her.

Maile didn't have to see it to know what the letter said. She shook her head. "Sorry, Dave, can't help you this time. Boyden's right in this. You *are* a minor and, without your parents' permission—or a guardian's—I should by rights kick you out of here right now. I'm not going to though, but after today you will not be allowed to even practice on this track without that letter, signed and in my possession."

He was clearly not pleased, but he nodded with good grace. "I'll get someone to sign it for me." Stuffing the envelope back in his breast pocket, he turned to go, only to be stopped by Maile's hand on his arm. His eyes went down to her hand, and then to her face.

"Not just *anyone,* Dave," she said, smiling to take the censuring edge off her tone. "It has to be either a *parent* or a *guardian.*"

"I'll get it signed"—he shrugged off her hand—"if it's the last thing I do," he muttered under his breath.

And then he was gone.

Maile went to the window and watched him as he returned to his crew and his car. He was angry. For a fleeting moment she wished she could disregard Boyden's advice and tell David that he could use the track anytime he wished to. But she couldn't.

Other boys began to arrive with their cars and their pit

crews, and they diverted Maile's thoughts from David's problems. She checked each car as it went past the tower. Today was only a practice day, a sort of "get acquainted" session for Maile's benefit.

The bleachers started filling up, mostly with friends of the drivers who had come to watch them compete with each other. There was no prize, so there was no pressure on any of the boys.

As the afternoon wore on, Maile's thoughts were often jarred by memories of other days spent at the speedway. Mike's ghost no longer haunted her, but his memory remained sweetly imbedded in her mind and heart. It was enough to make her wish she had had the heart to sell the speedway. . . .

She greeted the end of the day with a sense of relief. It was over; the ice had been broken and she had neither drowned nor gotten frostbite. Sliding one hand under her hair, she slowly massaged the knots at the back of her neck. She had not realized she had been so tense, but there it was: she heard the cracking sounds as she rubbed her neck, and smiled wearily. Thank goodness this was over.

Amid wolf whistles and shouted thanks for a wonderful afternoon, Maile went to her car and drove away from the speedway, grateful that Mike's friends were there to see that everything was cleaned up and the place locked.

The smell of fresh coffee greeted her as she stepped into her house about twenty minutes later. She smiled, feeling an immeasurable sense of joy at finding Jake in her kitchen.

"It's about time you came home," he said as he came to meet her at the kitchen door. "I'm starving."

Maile lifted her face for his kiss, wondering if she would ever see the day when her heart would not be in her throat

143

at the first sight of him. It was a lingeringly sweet kiss that left her wanting more. But he pushed her gently away, and reminded her that he was hungry.

"You're always hungry," she accused with a short laugh.

"Yeah, but this time it's for food." He ran a finger lightly across her chin, and then moved away. "I've got steak in the broiler, and the salad's in the fridge. Just vinegar and oil since you didn't have anything else in the house. . . ."

"If I had known—"

"No, darling, don't apologize. Being with you is all that counts." He smiled down at her. "And thanks for inviting me over."

Maile drew in her breath. "Oh, Jake!" In a flash she was in his arms. "I love you! Oh, if you only knew how very much I love you."

"I do know, Maile," he whispered, bending to kiss her warmly on the lips. "And I love you." His arms tightened, pulling her hard against him as his mouth came down to hers again. "I love you, Maile Riordan," he murmured against her eagerly parted lips.

Maile was floating on a soft, fluffy cloud. His admission of love had lifted a worrisome load from her mind and now she felt weightless. She answered his kiss with growing passion, no longer afraid to let him know that she was his to command.

A sizzling sound seemed to fill the room, and suddenly Jake pushed her away.

"Dammit, woman, you're making me burn our dinner," he growled huskily, pulling open the broiler door.

Maile wouldn't have known, or cared, if the steaks had

burned. Her mind was on Jake's sweet avowal of love, and she neither saw nor tasted what she ate.

"Was Arthur at the track today?" Jake's voice seemed to come from a great distance. Maile blinked, trying to focus her eyes on his face. She smiled crookedly—she had had too much wine.

"I didn't see him, Jake." She shook her head and closed her eyes briefly. "I wouldn't have known him even if I'd seen him, love. I don't know your nephew."

"Sure, you do," he murmured. He reached out for the bottle of wine and again filled her glass. "Tall, good-looking kid, a little on the skinny side—drink your wine, sweetheart—kinda shaggy right now; he needs a haircut."

"Sounds like *The Shaggy Dog* movie," she tittered, her hand going out for her wineglass. "Honestly, darling, can't you describe the boy a little better?" she chided, taking the glass to her lips.

"Don't you sign them in or something like that?" he asked, his voice so quiet, she had to strain to hear.

"Of course, we do. But there was no Arthur signing in." She took sip after sip of wine, stalling for time, trying desperately to remember all the names on the racing register.

"No . . . no Arthur," she stated firmly. "Honestly, Jake, he wasn't there."

"Blond hair, longish sideburns," he insisted, filling her glass again. "He used to laugh a lot before he and I started hassling about this stupid notion he has of racing." His eyes roamed over her face, taking in the flush caused by the wine, the confused expression in her green eyes, the gentle curve of her smiling lips. "Maybe around you he still does."

145

Maile shook her head. "No, don't know him," she said emphatically.

Jake's gaze dropped to his plate and, working his remaining food around the plate with his fork, he continued grilling her. Maile fielded his questions as best as she could, never realizing until it was too late that no matter what she said he did not believe that she did not know Arthur.

"Is this inquisition over?" she demanded angrily, pushing away from the table. "Because even if it isn't, I'm through answering questions." Legs shaky with the effects of the wine, Maile took her dishes to the sink, ran water over them, and then started out of the kitchen, only to be stopped by Jake barring the exit.

"If you were in a position to be with Arthur—like family, say—would you obey me unquestioningly and not interfere in my dealings with him?"

Maile felt the flush heightening in her cheeks, anger swiftly erasing all other emotion. "Even my own father I never obeyed *unquestioningly,*" she snapped.

"And why I would want to interfere in your dictatorship over your nephew, I don't know, but you seem to be suffering under the delusion that I am dying to do just that." Furiously she tossed her head, then squeezed past him and hurried into the living room.

Jake started to follow her, but froze when he heard the phone ringing. And then Maile's voice: bright, friendly, *warmer* than it had ever been to him.

"Ah, Mickey! No, you're not interrupting anything. . . . What? Oh, of course, you nut!" She laughed, a tingling, delighted laugh that thrust through Jake's form like a knife.

Maile hung up the phone and allowed her smile to fade.

146

Even though Mickey could not have seen her frowns, she had forced a smile to her lips while she spoke to him, still a firm believer that a smile had the power to go through the lines.

So I'm a nut! she thought. In a burst of activity she picked up a towel she'd left earlier draped across a chair and started dusting Mike's trophies, her thoughts on the man still in her kitchen. Though slightly tipsy, she nevertheless understood that Jake had been surreptitiously giving her a guardianship test, and she'd failed miserably. Her mouth drooped.

Jake watched her from the kitchen doorway, his eyes smoldering with anger, yet still nothing compared to the fury that burned in the core of his being. His eyes went past her to the trophy in her hand, brilliant, intense, glinting like sapphires in the sun. He suddenly felt as though a knife had been plunged into his heart and was being ruthlessly twisted.

It was something Jake Weston had never felt before in his life, this all-consuming jealousy that tore at his insides. Good God, he was jealous of a dead man! The knife was twisted more, and he realized it wasn't just Mike Sloan's memory that stood between him and Maile—there were all the others who were constantly on the phone to her, calling her to come to them, luring her away from him.

His large bronzed hand closing over her wrist stopped her abruptly. Maile turned, her eyes blazing fire. "What? You're still here?" Wrenching her hand free of his hold, she turned fully to face him. "I thought you'd left, Jake. That's usually what little boys do when they start losing the game—pick up their marbles and go home."

He stood very still for one breathless moment. "Is that what you think I am, Maile?" Reaching out, he curved his hand around her neck, drawing her to him. "Does this feel like a little boy's kiss?" He covered her mouth with an urgent need to punish; Maile dimly recognized this and stood unmoving in his arms.

"And this?" he rasped out, pressing himself against her, letting her feel his body's arousal. Maile's already reeling senses spun dizzyly; she felt the floor moving under her.

"No, Jake," she begged almost inaudibly. As if he hadn't heard her, his need to master her pushing him to the edge of insanity, he bent farther, lifting her in his arms as he straightened.

Fighting against her own rising desire for him, Maile pushed as hard as she could against the chest against which she was pressed so urgently, but her struggles were futile.

Later—much, much later—Maile awoke to find Jake's side of the bed obnoxiously empty. She felt the tears fill her eyes, then they started slipping out of the corners, running down to dampen her hair.

"Oh, Mike!" she groaned brokenly. "What have I done? Oh, God, what have I done!" She felt crawly all over with self-disgust, and worst of all, *cheap*, as the camera in her mind replayed the drama recently enacted in her bed. There'd been no tenderness, no genuine love expressed as Jake had taken her. And she had responded wildly, shamelessly, driven by some demon inside her that shut off all thought but that of the man who could quench the thirst that was like a living thing inside her.

She couldn't get into the shower fast enough, turning on the cold water full blast, ignoring the shivers that shot through her as the pelting rain assailed her. Hands trembling, she soaped her body, unconsciously seeking to wash away all trace of him.

Never again! she swore in her mind as she turned off the shower and stepped out into the beauty of her black and gold bathroom. Grabbing the towel off the rack, she dried herself swiftly, then padded back into her bedroom to dress. Never! No, never again would she let Jake use her like that.

What was she going to do? she asked herself as she dressed in faded jeans and a sweat shirt left shapeless from the many washings it had had through the years. Where did she think she would go in the middle of the night? Anywhere. . . . For a ride . . . for a long walk . . . just away from the house until this wretched feeling, festering like a cancer inside her, eased off.

Half an hour later Maile sat in a booth at an all-night restaurant, a half-full cup of coffee growing cold in front of her, and stared unseeing out the window. In her mind, Jake's words hammered unmercifully: "If you were in a position to be with Arthur—like family, say—would you obey me unquestioningly and not interfere in my dealings with him?"

A weight settled on her shoulders, making them droop with defeat and disappointment. Whether or not he married her, or even continued seeing her, had hinged on her answer to that miserable question.

"More coffee?" the waitress asked above her, breaking into Maile's sour thoughts. Startled, Maile glanced down at her coffee and saw that the cup was still almost full.

She shook her head. "I've had enough." In more ways than one, she said to herself.

Maile had a depressing week. But it seemed that the more wretched she felt, the better her designs were. Both

Janey and Ginny commented upon this, and were barked at for their insolence.

"Mrs. Pannell is on the phone, Maile," Janey hollered from the showroom.

Maile dropped the sketch she had been studying, groaning softly as she left the chair upon which she had been sitting all morning.

"Pannell," she repeated, too tired to even think which client this was.

Grimacing, she picked up the phone, telling herself she could not handle even one more client. Not unless one of the other ones dies, she affirmed in her mind. But when Joyce Pannell told her she had a wedding group to outfit, Maile saw dollar signs swimming in front of her eyes and readily agreed to take on the job. The sooner she amassed a fortune, the sooner she could pay Jake off and stand on equal footing with him.

"You did it again," Janey accused the moment Maile returned to the workroom. She wrinkled her nose. "You took another order." Brown eyes narrowed speculatively, she moved closer to Maile, frowning. "Are you sure you're all right, Maile?" she asked, her quiet tone edged with concern.

"Yes. Why do you ask?" Maile's mouth twitched at the corners.

Janey smiled sadly. "You're driving yourself as though you had the hounds of Hell at your heels. You're just taking on too much at once, Maile."

Maile shrugged. "If you don't think we can do it, I will call Mrs. Pannell and cancel on her, Janey." Her tone clearly expressed her indifference. *I don't really care,* she finished in her mind.

"Oh, we can do it, all right," Janey retorted. "The

question is, can you hold up under the strain?" Her brown eyes roamed over Maile's slender form. "I don't think you're even eating right, let alone resting right." Her eyes noted the dark circles under her friend's eyes.

"I'm all right," Maile said, and went back to work.

It was TGIF day, Ginny announced as she sailed through the back door a couple of hours later, followed shortly thereafter by Janey, who cautioned Maile against working too late again.

"You've got a race tomorrow, remember that!" she called out over her shoulder.

As though I could forget, Maile thought resignedly. David had reminded her last night when he had dropped by to give her his guardian's signed authorization for him to compete in tomorrow's race.

Jay Arthur, 314 North Palo Verde Drive, Gilroy, California. The name and address were indelibly etched on the insides of Maile's tired lids; she could see it even now. And she should be happy for David, but she could only think that she and Jake had quarreled over a boy who was not even in the competition.

Several hours later Maile collapsed onto a kitchen chair, feeling completely defeated, facing an unappetizing dinner, and wondering why she had not stopped at a hamburger joint. Anything would have been better than eating at home . . . alone.

Sensing where her thoughts were taking her, she threw her dinner in the garbage can, washed her dishes, and went in to take her bath.

Curling up with a good book, she was asleep within minutes and, gratefully, awoke the next morning unable to recall what—if anything—she had dreamed.

Today was the day—"the biggee," as David had called

151

it: the race that would determine the winner between the college group and the high school group. Smiling sheepishly, he had admitted that the high schoolers had among them some "good drivers who'll give us a run for our money."

Donning jeans and a cowl-neck blue sweater, she sat down at her vanity. Her hair went up in a braided coronet. Applying a pale lip gloss, she decided to forgo the little makeup she normally wore, and left the house.

George Mason met her at the gate, dressed in white coveralls and wearing a grin that immediately put Maile at her ease.

"Dean's going to be your announcer," he told her. "He said he'd meet you up at the tower." His gray-blue eyes twinkled merrily. "Has a surprise for you."

I'll watch half the race, then go home, she promised herself. A good night's rest was what she needed to chase away the doldrums. Hunching her shoulders to ease the tension that had settled between her shoulder blades, she went up to the tower, wondering what Dean was up to this time.

Her head bowed, she did not see her brother watching her from the window, and stood for a stunned moment, too disbelieving of her own eyesight to greet him when he opened the door for her.

"Bryan!" Laughing softly, she threw herself into his arms. "Oh, it's been so long! I've missed you!"

"I've missed you too." He held her away from him, and looked her over. "You're prettier, but a little too thin.

"I take it that you've conquered Mike's ghost?" he asked, looking away from her to the track.

Maile took a moment to study him. Aside from a few new wrinkles around his eyes, he had not changed.

152

"Yes. And you? How are you and Seattle getting along?"

He made a so-so movement with his hand. "It rains an awful lot, but I think I'm going to survive." He grinned.

Maile picked up the list of entries and ran a quick eye over the names. "I—" She started, but he interrupted her.

"I see you removed Mike's name from the gate."

Maile nodded. "Mike's friends convinced me he was going to change it anyway. Chuck said Mike had talked about calling it the Seacliff Speedway. I asked some of the others, and they confirmed it."

"And Weston?" There was a sharp edge in his tone that went through Maile like a cold shiver.

She cleared her throat, nervously. "He's still in the picture, Bryan," she said, adding silently, "at least as far as the business goes." Sighing, she turned away from his scrutiny. "We haven't made any money—and even when we do, we won't have enough to do more than skim a thin layer off the bale of loot we owe him." Her voice was tinged with irritation, and she wished he had not brought Jake into the conversation.

Bryan stared morosely out the window as Maile turned on the mike to announce that it was time for the racers to bring their cars into a line in front of the tower.

"In case you're wondering why we're doing it this way, just ask George, who'll be coming round to do the tech inspection. Have your driver's license ready."

There was an excited flurry below. The girls who had been flirting with the drivers sprinted across the track to take their places either atop the roofs of their cars or in the bleachers. Within moments the track was clear.

Maile turned to Bryan and found him staring down, his eyes narrowed in thought. She followed the line of his gaze, expecting to find a girl waving up at him, but instead found David looking up at her. The sun-streaked hair was being whipped about by the wind, but it didn't seem to bother him in the least. He was grinning confidently.

"What's wrong, Bry?"

"That kid, the one waving to you. I think I know him."

Maile turned and looked down at David. "You mean David?" She waved, smiling widely.

"Is that his name?"

"Yes. David Arthur."

Bryan seemed puzzled. "Are you sure? I could've almost sworn . . ." He shook his head. "I guess I mistook him for someone who used to work for Weston."

Maile laughed. "Not hardly. He's too young. Besides, he's been in school all along, working summers for his father's family." She smiled, thinking of the many times *she* had been mistaken for someone else.

"Maile, do you have a couple o' thousand lying around that you could lend me?"

Maile's smile faded. "Two thousand dollars! Good God, Bryan, what in the world do you do with your money? You spend more in a week than I do all month!" She immediately regretted her reaction when she saw the crestfallen expression on his face.

"I—I'm sorry, Bry," she said lamely. "I shouldn't have said that. It's just that I'm tired." Was she ever! Particularly of doling out money.

His morose, defeated expression tugged at her heart, and she knew she would move heaven and earth to remove that bleak look from his eyes. "If I have it, I'll give it to you, but you'll have to wait until Monday for me to go to the bank."

He made an annoyed cluck with his tongue. "I can't wait, Maile, I need it today, right now."

His words, coupled with the sober expression on his dear face, brought a chill to her spine. Was he in some kind of trouble again? Was he gambling? She lifted her eyes to his face, but his expression was unchanged.

"You could write me a check," he suggested lightly, keeping his eyes on the track.

"I don't have enough in my personal account, Bry," she said impatiently. "You'll just have to wait until Monday."

He sighed, and the suggestion of a shrug broke the strained set of his broad shoulders. "I can't wait until Monday, Maile. I'm going back to Seattle tonight. You see, I'm—I'm getting married."

"Married?!" Maile had forgotten to turn off the mike and now the word echoed all around the speedway. Embarrassed, she fumbled with the switch and turned off the mike. "Married?" she repeated disbelievingly. "When? And to whom?"

Bryan was digging through his wallet, and brought out a picture of a girl with long blond hair and large blue eyes. She had a petulant look about her, Maile thought, and decided she did not like her future sister-in-law's looks.

"I suppose she's in Seattle, waiting for you with bated breath," she said spitefully, wondering if the blonde was the reason Bryan was so desperate both to get the two thousand dollars and himself back to Seattle.

He shifted uncomfortably from one foot to the other. "As a matter of fact, she's in San Francisco visiting with friends of hers."

"Oh?" she said with her chin tilted upward in a manner that had always put Bryan on the defensive. "How come you didn't bring her with you so that I could meet her?"

Bryan gave her an uneasy grin, and shifted positions again. "She didn't want to come with me."

I wonder why, Maile thought grimly. Perhaps it was because the dizzy little blonde was doing a number on Bryan and she was afraid Maile would see through it? There was a tiny but undeniable vindictive streak in her, and for a moment Maile considered refusing Bryan the loan to revenge herself against the girl for the slight.

She sighed in resignation. She couldn't hurt Bryan. "I'll write you a check, Bry, then go deposit some money into my account." She pulled out her purse from a cabinet behind them. "And you don't have to pay me back," she added, knowing he wouldn't anyway. "You can consider it your wedding present," she finished softly as she wrote out the check.

For a few moments he just looked down at her with something akin to pity in his eyes. Maile stared back, her eyes taking in every loving detail of his face, knowing it would be a long time before she saw him again once he married.

"Be careful, won't you, Bry?" she pleaded, standing up on her toes to kiss him on the cheek.

"You know I will," he whispered, holding her close. He kissed her on the cheek, and then reluctantly pushed her away. "And you," he added, gently tweaking her nose, "you take care of yourself and watch out for all those wolves." He was casual enough, but Maile sensed the underlying strain in his voice. It worried her.

"Be careful, Bry," she beseeched.

He nodded; then he turned and went out the door.

Clamping her lower lip between her teeth, Maile stood for a moment with her eyes closed to stem the tears that threatened behind them. She took a deep breath and forced her attention to the business at hand, trying to forget that when Bryan closed the door behind him, he had closed another chapter of their lives. The roar of his car was drowned out by the revving of engines and the cheers going up as each of the boys received the official go-ahead.

The drivers climbed into their cars as George Mason moved away; they strapped themselves in, pulled on their crash helmets and gloves, and waited to be told to move on to the starting line.

Maile saw Dean Reynolds coming up with a reporter and left the tower to them in favor of sitting on the bleachers with the other spectators. George Mason was a fine manager; if anything was needed, he was there to take care of it.

The flagman, wearing a white suit and standing close enough to the track to be seen by the drivers but far enough away to be safe, stood with his flag poised. The spring breeze drifted gently over the sun-bathed, silent cars. The fans were hushed, and waited breathlessly to see the green flag going down.

The flag came down, sending the cars on their way. The cars roared loudly across the starting line, *swish, swish, swish,* all the way down the line until the last car was across.

Maile found herself almost fearfully following David's green car, again wishing he had not chosen Mike's colors. American racing people considered green unlucky, but Mike, being originally from England, had not cared that he was flying in the face of tradition.

The sun went behind the clouds, and for a few moments Maile lost sight of David's car. At the precise moment that the sun came away from the clouds, something went

157

wrong with the green car with the broad yellow stripe. Maile stood up, her heart in her throat, and watched him in hypnotic horror as he headed unerringly toward the wall. She closed her eyes tightly; she did not want to see him crash.

Coward! Startled as though she had really heard a voice taunting her, Maile opened her eyes and found, to her supreme relief, that David had corrected and was there in third place, in the inside lane. She sat down; rather she collapsed onto the bench because her knees had turned to jelly.

If that slight error had frightened him, David was no longer afraid. It showed in the way he maneuvered his car around the car in second place. For the next few laps he seemed content to crowd the car in front of him. He seemed to be biding his time, although the man in first place, driving a red and white Camaro, was staying a steady ten seconds ahead of him. In the meantime the third-place car, a yellow Mustang, was pressing him.

Fifteen teams had entered. Only nine had made the race; out of those nine, one had dropped out early on because of a blown tire. Four of the cars were in what appeared to be a huddle, while the fifth car had pulled away only seconds before and was pressing the yellow Mustang following David.

There were only two laps remaining when David made his move around the first-place car. He took the lead and kept it.

A wild roar of cheering came from the bleachers as David came around for the last time.

And then the race was ended, and David was bringing his car into a grassy patch between the pits where his crew was waiting, along with George and the reporter friend of

Dean's. A photographer joined the group, and then the young girls started climbing down from the bleachers to go crowd around him.

Smiling, David hoisted himself out of his car without bothering to open the door, and leaned against his car. Slowly he pulled off his helmet, handing it to one of his crew, then removed a glove and ran a careless hand through his sweat-dampened tawny locks.

George Mason moved up to him with a microphone, congratulated him, and awarded him his trophy. David chuckled into the mike and thanked George for the award.

"You earned it, son," Maile heard George say. "That was some good driving!"

Holding the shiny trophy up in a salute, David turned to search for Maile, found her, and waved his prize, his mouth wide with a triumphant grin. Maile waved back, but remained where she was. He had a number of girls rushing to congratulate him, and his crew of four already gathered around him; he didn't need her too.

Slowly she made her way down from the bleachers, then threaded a path through the departing crowd to her car. She smiled as she opened the door and climbed in. Rank indeed had its privileges. Being the owner of the Seacliff Speedway allowed her to park wherever she wanted, and being Mike's protégée had taught her to park some distance from the parking area. So while everyone was trying to back up, or turn around, she got on the road and was already on the highway before the crowd started weaving out of the parking lot.

It was almost seven when she pulled into her own driveway. Her heart literally skipped a beat when she saw Jake's car parked on the street, between her house and Janice's. Suddenly she was no longer tired, no longer plagued by memories of what she had tried to convince herself had been better days. Jake had not forgotten her.

Smiling, she left her car, locked the door, then almost ran up to the porch. Her spirits began to droop when she found her front door still locked, then hit rock-bottom when she went into the house and there was no one to greet her. Against her conscious effort her thoughts went to other times when she was late getting home: those times her neighbor Janice had been more than happy to let Jake wait at her house; and Jake had eagerly accepted, even though Maile had long ago given him a key to her house.

Maile went back to her porch, her stomach tied in knots with jealousy, and looked across her hedge to her neighbor's house. Her eyes picked out a faint golden glow in the room she knew Janice used as her bedroom since her husband had left her. Except for that light, the entire house was in darkness.

Knowing how Janice felt about anything wearing pants, she did a slow burn. It was no wonder Jake felt no real desire to be married. He could always get what he wanted without it, she thought disparagingly. There were the Janices of the world, who gave *any* man what he wanted because it satisfied their own biological urges, or because such a relationship brought them desired material things. She smiled ruefully. And then there were the foolish ones —the Mailes—who gave a man what he wanted because they loved unwisely.

Sniffing away tears that were determined to fall, she went back into the house, hoping in a small corner of her heart that Jake would eventually come to her. Her pride was at such a low ebb that she would have invited him in—no questions asked, no accusations made. But Jake did not come, and she saw the futility of waiting for him.

160

Reality had to be faced: Jake had found a more compatible companion in Janice. Maile left the sofa where she had spent the worst hour of her entire life waiting for Jake, and went to bed.

Perhaps it was for the best, she told herself as she crawled into her warm waterbed. For Jake at any rate. Janice had nothing to do with any speedway—she would pose no threat with his precious nephew unless she proved to be as unscrupulous as Maile thought her, and she decided to seduce the boy. . . .

CHAPTER 9

By morning Maile had wrapped herself in a protective shell and convinced herself that she could survive without Jake Weston. Her breakfast had been consumed while reviewing a fashion magazine, and now the dishes were in the drainer, waiting to be put away.

Dressed in tight jeans and a blue chambray shirt, she started doing what she knew she should have done weeks ago. Taking an empty carton from her garage, she started filling it with Mike's trophies and pictures to put in storage until Mike's friends built the display room at the speedway.

She heard the rumble of Jake's Ferrari, but she couldn't be sure that it was not stopping at Janice's house. She tried not to care as she continued with her chore, carefully cleaning and wrapping each picture and trophy before committing it to the box.

A heavy knock sounded on her door, startling Maile as she was gazing at a picture of Mike holding up a trophy while she looked down at him from the roof of his car. She almost dropped the picture in her haste to place it in the box.

"Who is it?"

"Jake. Open the damn door!"

Pride stiffened her carriage as she went to the door and opened it. She stood aside to let Jake pass into the room and immediately realized it was a mistake. She should have kept him outside on the porch, making him tell her what he wanted before letting him in.

"Now that the damn door is open. . . ." She attempted to inject humor into her tone, but failed miserably.

He turned to look at her, a cold smile—if one could call it a smile—on his lips and an unreadable expression in his eyes. Maile stiffened with apprehension.

He closed the distance between them, and held out a folded newspaper. "You must be very proud of yourself now," he jeered.

Maile looked at him, not at the paper, in sharp surprise and confusion. "Why? Because the speedway's finally open?"

"The speedway," he minced as though the very words were obscene. "If I'd had any sense at all, I'd have known you meant trouble the first time I laid eyes on you." He shook his head in a disbelieving way. "If I'd known then what I know now about you, I'd have conned you into giving me more authority over that damn speedway, and promptly had it closed!"

It was only then that Maile thought to unfold the paper, and looked at it curiously, wondering what it could contain to make Jake so angry with her. She found David grinning up at her, one hand holding his trophy, the other lifted in silent salute.

"Arthur Muccia." Though she said the name, her mind would not accept it. He was *David*! *David Arthur*! Her friend. And a friend did not lie to a friend. A friend did not give a friend a false name.

"So this is your nephew," she said, managing somehow to keep her voice from betraying the sadness that erupted in her breast. She wanted to cry.

"Don't pretend this is the first time you've seen him!" Maile could hear the sarcasm crackling in his voice as the words were flung at her head.

"I'm not pretending, Jake. And I wasn't lying to you before when I said I didn't know your nephew. I knew him, all right, but as David Arthur."

"Do you really expect me to believe that?" he ground out savagely. "Arthur would never hide behind an alias. He has always been proud of his father—if anything, too damn proud," he muttered disgustedly. "His father was Federico Muccia of Grand Prix fame. Your boyfriend knew him well—they were two of a kind." His lip curled with disdain, and it was then that Maile began to understand why Jake hated racers and anything and anybody associated with the sport.

Federico Muccia. Mike had introduced her to him in Spain. The great Federico—one of the great philanderers. But why should all racers—why should *she*!—pay for whatever Muccia might have done to Jake's sister?

Maile unconsciously lifted her chin. "Believe me or not, Jake; it's your prerogative. But I honestly did not know that David was your nephew. . . ." She allowed her voice to trail off as she took note of the doubt in his eyes. He had closed his mind against believing her. He had it firmly imbedded in his brain that if Mike had known who David was, Maile, too, would have known.

164

Talk about adding two and two and coming up with five! she thought furiously. "Not that it would have made that much difference, Jake. I didn't think you had any right to keep your nephew from racing and I still don't, whether his name is David or Arthur."

"Your honesty is very refreshing," he sneered.

Maile winced under the impact of his sarcasm and thrust out her chin even farther. "At least I've been honest with you, Jake, and that's a lot more than I can say for you."

"I've been nothing if not honest with you, Maile," he countered, taking a step closer to her. "But *you*! 'I love you, Jake,' " he mimicked. "While all the time, behind my back, you were encouraging Arthur to defy me."

Maile shook her head in defeat. She could talk till she was blue in the face, and this man would never believe her. With hard-fought calm she went across the room and sat down on the big leather chair by the window.

"You have nothing to say to me, Maile?" His voice was so cold, so withdrawn that Maile cringed. She knew even before he spoke again that his next words would cut through her with calculated severity.

And he did not disappoint her. "I guess, then, Maile, there's nothing left . . . except to say good-bye."

He turned and walked away, out into the day that had suddenly lost its brightness, leaving Maile to stare after him with teary eyes.

Time slipped by slowly as she sat staring out the window, her mind vascillating between feeling sorry for herself because she feared she had lost Jake for good, and being angry with the one who had caused her this grief. Her anger won out.

How could David do that to her? She had trusted him,

and he had deceived her. *How could he!* The sentence echoed again and again in her mind.

"Ah, Jake," she breathed. Foolishly she still hoped that once he had cooled down, he would come back to her.

But what if he didn't? nagged her inner self. What would she do then? Crawl on her hands and knees to him and beg forgiveness? Something twisted with repulsion in her midsection, and she knew she could not, would not, go begging to him.

Unable to sit there letting her thoughts drag her into the well of despair that even Mike's death had failed to do, Maile went into the bathroom to take a bath. She was suddenly very weary, but this she attributed to the strain she had been under lately, and the heavy workload she had forced on herself.

She walked stiffly through her bedroom, keeping her eyes averted, unable to bear the sight of her bed and the memories this would evoke. Slipping off her clothes while the tub filled with hot sudsy water, she wondered what she could do the rest of the day.

She stepped into the tub and brought all her concentration to bear on easing the tension that felt like a ball of fire between her shoulder blades.

A vision of herself lying in Jake's muscular arms flashed unannounced—and unwanted—before her eyes, and she cringed. She shivered with remembrances, and closed her eyes as though that tiny action would close off her mind; would make it unresponsive to the memories that had intruded into her conscious thoughts.

Why did I have to remember! Maile stood up swiftly and turned on the shower, cursing her body for making her mind remember those long, lean hands that delighted in caressing the pliant skin that even now tingled with remembered pleasure.

It was appraisal time, she told herself as she turned off the shower and stepped out of the tub. The speedway was operating well under George Mason's direction; Janey and Ginny had run the boutique without her before and could do so again. Bryan was in Seattle, married to his blond snob. There was nothing to hold her to Watsonville. *Nothing.* Even the word held no substance. Maile started to sag, then promptly stiffened her backbone.

Quickly donning jeans and a shirt, she left the bathroom, telling herself she could dry and curl her hair later. Right now, it was more important that she call Pat and Jim in Nevada to ask if they could put up with her for a few days; she badly needed a change of scenery.

She had already dialed the area code for Tonopah when her doorbell rang. Frowning, she glanced over her shoulder at the door, wondering who it could be that was so insistent to gain admission. Sighing, she put down the phone and went to answer the door.

"Oh, it's you," she said, her tone ungracious, the look in her eyes eloquently expressing her annoyance at finding David at her door.

"Don't, Maile." His hands went down and grabbed hers. Maile made no move to loosen his grip, and he relaxed his hold.

"Lord, Maile, if I could undo what I've done . . . believe me, I would do anything you say if it would put things to rights with us again.

"I'm sorry, Maile," he whispered. His hands let go of hers, went up and cupped around her chin, lifting her face to his. "If I had had the slightest inkling that what I was doing would end up hurting *you,* I would've—" He could not continue. His eyes filled, and his face grew red with embarrassment.

"Oh, Maile, I'm so sorry!" he cried, and with a noise that was almost a sob, he threw his arms around her and buried his head on her shoulder. A great shudder rippled through his tall slender frame, communicating itself to her.

Maile could not remain angry with him. "David, it's all right," she whispered soothingly. Somehow she managed to get an arm wedged between them, and lightly touched his face, urging him to lift his head.

"It's not your fault . . . what happened between Jake and me." Very gently she disentangled herself and stepped back. She laughed hoarsely, wiping her face with the backs of her hands to dry the tears that had slipped past her guard.

"Listen to me. I keep calling you David. But it's hard to think of you as Arthur," she apologized, turning to him with a smile trembling on her lips.

His eyes gazed wonderingly into hers, and he smiled. "I didn't lie about that, Maile. My name *is* David—Arturo Davidde Muccia—though the Westons would prefer to have me be just Arthur Weston," he finished bitterly.

"I see."

"No, I don't think you do, Maile," he contradicted, his tone quiet, a trifle brooding. He walked past her and plopped down on the sofa, crossing his feet and leaning back against the soft cushions.

Maile stood by the door, waiting for him to enlarge upon his statement. But David didn't seem to be in any hurry to continue.

"You want something to drink?" she asked, moving

toward the kitchen. *Even if you don't, I* need *something.* Her throat felt raspy, and it ached.

"I could stand a cup of coffee, if you've got some," he said, getting up and following her into the kitchen.

Straddling a kitchen chair, David began to explain. "It started a long time ago, Maile, long before my mother even met my father." His lips curled with cynical amusement. "Imagine in this day and age. . . . The Westons had my mom earmarked for some rich dude from England; someone with a title, no less. Mom didn't care for things like that—as a matter of fact, neither does Jake—but the old folks were set on having their daughter 'marry well,' you know? Then Mom went with a girl friend to a race in Paris, and my dad saw her. She was so pretty, he said, that he couldn't help but rush her.

"Anyway . . . some nine months later I came around." His eyes watered, and he looked away in embarrassment. "The Westons never forgave my dad. You see, he was already married. The Westons pulled rank on Mom—she was still a minor, you see—and brought her back home. But she ran away again and went back to my dad. And for a few years they managed somehow, but my grandparents would not even acknowledge my existence. Except for Jake, Mom didn't see any of her relatives until after Grandpa died. Then Grandma—I guess she felt lonely for her daughter—invited us to come spend one Christmas with her.

"I guess my dad misunderstood what was happening." He took the mug Maile offered him, curling his long fingers around it. For a moment he just stared down at the steam coming from the coffee, then took a small sip and continued. "Anyway, he told my mom she could return to her family if she wanted to, but he would not let me go.

169

Mom was as stubborn as Jake is, or maybe even more. She exploded. She told him that I was *her* son, and hers alone, and she would take me wherever she damn well pleased. Dad watched us go, then went out on an all-night binge." He laughed huskily.

"Mom got as far as the airport with me, then changed her mind and went back home. She thought she would surprise Dad. Boy, did she ever! Dad had gone out and found himself someone to keep him warm while Mom was away. Mom hit the roof, and Dad stormed out of the house and stayed gone for months.

"Mom finally got tired of waiting for him to come back, and brought me here to my grandmother.

"They were—they were trying to effect a reconciliation when Dad got killed."

Maile recalled Mike telling her about the accident that had killed Muccia and injured three other racers, including Mike. If memory served, Muccia had been in the company of a voluptuous redhead when he died. *That* hardly added credence to Dave's belief that Federico had been in favor of a reconciliation with his common-law wife. A shudder rippled through her, and Maile quickly curved her fingers around her cup, taking it to her lips to stop their trembling.

"Mom made Jake promise that he would not let me follow in my dad's footsteps," he added after a while. "Jake promised readily, and ever since Mom died, he has done everything in his power to discourage me from going to the races—even as a spectator.

"That's why I couldn't tell you that he was my uncle, Maile," he said, grasping her hand agitatedly. "I was sure that he would lean on you hard if he ever found out that you were letting me use the track. I—I didn't think you could stand up to him," he finished apologetically, letting out his breath in a drawn-out sigh.

Neither did he, Maile thought, but there was no glory in knowing that Jake had not made her bow to his demands.

Maile stood up abruptly, and taking her cup to the sink, ran water over it. Then she busied herself in the kitchen, preparing dinner for the two of them. There was no reason to feel sorry for herself, she told herself firmly, willing her tears to stop burning behind her eyes. Given the chance to do it over, she would do things exactly as she had done them before: make the same mistakes, laugh at the same things, cry over the same things, send Jake away one night, and beg him to love her another.

Over dinner David begged her to let him stay with her. He could not go back to Jake's house—or rather, he *would* not. After a long and thorough discussion he finally convinced her that she should allow him to use her spare bedroom.

Later, while lying in her bed, unable to sleep, Maile thought over what she had agreed to do, and knew without the slightest twinge of doubt that when Jake heard about their living arrangements, he would zoom down from San Francisco and drag the poor kid home.

Jake "zoomed" slower in reality than he did in Maile's mind. It took him an entire week to discover that his nephew was no longer at the university, and then another three days to figure out where he had gone. And then he swooped down upon the hapless two like a dark, avenging angel—and without warning.

In the meantime Maile had allowed herself to fall into a false sense of security. She had just stepped out of her bath and was wrapping a bath towel around her shivering body when David called out from the front room that he had just made a fresh pot of coffee. Wrapping another towel around her dripping hair, Maile padded out to the kitchen for a cup. Feeling entirely at ease with David after falling all over him for the past few days, she saw nothing wrong in being with him in her state of undress. She sat down and took a cookie from the plate David had set in the center of the kitchen table.

"A charming little scene," said a voice that was dripping with sarcasm, a voice that she had both dreaded and hoped to hear. Turning, Maile found Jake framed in the kitchen door, a murderous look on his face.

Maile found it impossible to speak, and felt like a complete idiot sitting there in her towel, her eyes like saucers riveted to his scowling face.

After that one barbed comment, Jake totally ignored Maile and turned his attention to David, freezing him to the spot as he had started to leave the room.

Threats the like of which she had never thought to hear from an intelligent man like Jake tumbled from his lips with the velocity and dispassion of an automaton programmed for just such a function.

David stood staring at his uncle, giving no evidence of inner turmoil except the clenching of his fists at his sides as Jake continued his diatribe with rapier-sharp words that were edged with contempt. His gaze was fixed on Jake's face, and if Jake had not been seeing everything through angry eyes, Maile thought, he might have recognized that the boy was no longer listening to him.

Maile's eyes slid over Jake's frame, and her breath caught in her throat. She turned away, unable to look at him and unwilling to turn back to David.

172

Maile had thought it best not to interfere in their familial squabbles, yet she rose quickly to her feet and turned on Jake when she heard him say that he had expected *her* to "know better."

"With regard to what, Jake?" she demanded, her eyes glittering with rising fury.

"To this!" he bellowed. "I thought I could trust *you*. I thought—" He stopped abruptly, and stared down at her as though he were seeing her for the first time.

Impossible! said her doubting mind, but it seemed that for a moment Jake had sagged as he took in her appearance.

"Just what the hell has been going on here?" he snarled. His hands went out, grasped her by the shoulders and hauled her roughly out of the chair and toward him. "Just how much comfort have you been to the boy?" His fingers tightened painfully, his nails, short though they were, dug into her skin until Maile felt like screaming. He seemed crazed.

She was so intent on the pain he was inflicting—and the wild look in his eyes—that the accusation behind his words did not immediately sink into her mind. David, however, had no problem comprehending what his uncle meant.

"How dare you insinuate such a thing!" he screamed, his eyes blazing furiously into Jake's tight-jawed expression. "If you weren't so damn—"

"Don't you swear at me, boy!" Jake's fingers tightened even more on Maile's shoulders, making her cry out.

"Let me go, Jake, you're hurting me," she begged, moving up her hands to try and pry his fingers from her shoulders.

"You're despicable!" David spat out.

Jake laughed. It wasn't a pretty sound. Maile shivered in fear.

"Let me go, Jake!" She choked the words out, struggling against the long lean fingers that had once caressed her soft skin with a feather-soft touch.

He looked down at her, and this time Maile was almost certain that she saw pain in his eyes. His grip relaxed, but he did not release her.

"Tell me, lover, wouldn't you rather be made love to by a real man?" he murmured sarcastically, drawing her stiff body against him.

Maile heard David's gasp, and then strident footsteps took him out of the kitchen. Jake was too busy studying her flushed face to notice that David was no longer in the room. The slamming of the front door seemed to wake him from his daze, and he smiled sardonically.

"Let him go out and cool down," he said thickly. "He can't go anywhere—I've got his car blocked." Before Maile could anticipate his intention, he had bent down and had his mouth over hers. Maile felt her teeth pressing into her lip, and tasted something salty. *My own blood,* she thought as she struggled against him to get loose.

In her struggles she lost her towels. But before Jake could even think to take advantage of the situation, they heard a car being started outside.

"Damn that kid!" he bellowed. "He's hot-wired your car!"

At the moment Maile didn't care about her car. She knew she had only that brief moment when Jake was distracted to dash into her bedroom for her clothes. But she needn't have worried about Jake; he was too busy trying to keep David from driving away.

A few minutes later she came out to the porch and found Jake sitting on the bottom step.

"He's gone."

"Do you really blame him?"

Jake half turned to look at her and shrugged.

Five minutes later he had still not uttered a word. Maile was sitting on the porch swing, looking at his strong back, wondering what thoughts might be running through his mind.

"I can't wait for him forever," he finally said, rising to his feet. "When he comes back, Maile, I would appreciate it if you told him to go home. I don't want to get rough with either one of you, Maile, but that doesn't mean I won't."

Maile nodded glumly. She knew he would hurt *her* if David did not go home. And the only way he could hurt her anymore was through the speedway.

"He'll go home," she said wearily. "But only because I will tell him to go. And I'll tell him, Jake, not because I want him to go back to you, but because I know what mischief you can cause me." She felt her breath catch, and knew she had to go inside before she started crying. She slipped off the swing and was almost to the door when Jake stopped her.

"Maile, don't go in yet. I have something to tell you." He came up to the porch, close to her, but he made no move to touch her.

"In a few hours I'm going to go to Canada . . . to file charges against the secretary who made off with the money she conned your brother into transferring out of one of my dad's accounts." His hand moved up, cupped over her chin and lifted her face.

"Come with me, Maile. After we turn the woman over

175

to the proper authorities, we could grab a few days to get to really know each other. . . ."

Maile was taken aback, too surprised by what he'd said to react beyond thinking that Bryan would be happy to discover that the black cloud that had been hanging over him for the past few months was about to be lifted.

"Would you come with me, Maile? I need you with me."

Need. I need you with me. Not: Come with me, Maile, because I love you and want you with me.

"No," she said dully. "What you want—what you *need* me for— Those needs someone like Janice can satisfy with a lot more gusto than I ever could. Why don't you take her with you? I'm sure she'd love to go." Lifting her chin, she escaped his hold and stepped back.

Jake tightened his jaw angrily. "Remember—it was *you* I wanted," he said. He turned with purpose and left the porch.

Tears streaming unchecked down her suntanned cheeks, Maile stood on her porch and watched him walking across the lawn to Janice's house. She saw him knock on her door, then the door opened and he went in. Sobbing, Maile turned and ran back into her house, slamming the door behind her.

CHAPTER 10

Too nervous to stay indoors, Maile threw a cardigan across her shoulders and went for a walk. She eyed every car that she saw on her walk, praying it would be David returning so that she could give him Jake's message. The sooner he went home, the better off she would be.

She saw a police car coming toward her when she was nearly to her house—an unusual sight, for the neighborhood was quiet and seldom needed surveillance. Idly she watched it crawl up to the curb and stop in front of her house. Puzzled, she stood for a moment, staring at the policeman who left his car and started walking up to her porch. Now what? Maile asked herself. She moved swiftly toward her house, and reached her porch just as the policeman was lifting a hand to knock on her door.

"May I help you?" she asked.

The officer turned sharply on his heel and demanded, "Are you Maile Riordan?"

Maile could not explain why, but suddenly she felt frozen with fear. "I am Maile Riordan," she said.

"You own a Daytona Charger"—the officer consulted a pad he had drawn from his shirt pocket—"maroon, Rally wheels . . . license reading 'Sloan's'?"

A debilitating weakness struck Maile's knees, and for a sick moment she feared her legs would cave under her. But they held. "What about it?" she managed hoarsely.

"Your . . . nephew, I believe, had an accident earlier with it."

David! Maile's heart jerked painfully to her throat, and she reached out without thinking and grasped the officer's arm. "Where is he?" Her voice was reedy, and echoed eerily around her in the stillness of the night.

Dimly she heard the officer say that David had been taken to the hospital, but she did not hear him offering to take her to him in the squad car. She left him still talking, and flew across the yard into her neighbor's yard. She pounded on the door until Earleen answered. Sobbing, she begged to borrow a car. She had to get to David!

"Oh, Maile, John took the good car," Earleen answered sympathetically. "All that's left is that old relic of mine that you borrowed the last time you had yours in the shop." Her voice softened considerably. "You go on, I'll get you the keys. And calm yourself, honey, for goodness' sake!"

Distractedly as she ran to the Whites' garage, Maile thanked God for friends like Earleen and her husband, John.

Fifteen minutes later, by the grace of God and her own good driving habits, she arrived safely at the hospital.

Five minutes after that, she had found out where David

178

was, and found the doctor who had examined him in the emergency room.

Maile stared uncomprehendingly at the doctor. "Are you saying that unless you operate immediately, Dave might—" She shuddered, unable to say the word.

The doctor nodded, giving her a sympathetic smile. His wrinkled features spoke of many such confrontations in his career, yet the pained gleam in his eyes attested to the fact that the man was still bothered when he had to face concerned family members with unpleasant news.

Jake was the only one with the legal right to authorize the surgery, she thought, looking wildly about the hospital corridor, willing Jake to appear. She sagged. Jake was on his way to Canada, or already there.

"Where are the papers I need to sign?" she asked, her voice unnaturally quiet. She gave herself no time to think of what legal hassles she might be facing by lying about being the boy's guardian; at the moment she just didn't care. Getting him the medical aid he needed was the only thing that mattered.

After she signed the consent-for-surgery papers, the doctor went away, leaving Maile to choose between staying in his office or pacing in the waiting room. She opted for pacing. She knew she could not stay closed away in that small office, being so far away from David. Although she could do nothing to help him, she felt better just knowing she was on the same floor as he.

Damn Jake Weston! Anger directed at him because of his stubbornness, his stupidity where the boy was concerned, armed her with a small measure of courage, and she stiffened her backbone. David had to pull through—he just had to!

With all her heart Maile wished she could be certain

that David would be all right. But, perversely, her mind kept lapsing back to that other day several months back when she had waited long and pain-racked hours while the doctors tried to save Mike. At the end she had been too numb to understand when Dr. Reese had told her about all the complications that had set in, making it impossible for Mike to pull through. The only thing, she remembered, that had sunk in through the numbness was the doctor's assurance that, had Mike survived, he would have undoubtedly been an invalid. And she knew that Mike could never have been happy living like that.

With every footstep she heard, Maile cringed, and immediately sent her eyes to search the corridor, half hoping to find Jake walking toward her, half afraid it would be the doctor coming to tell her that they had lost David.

Time went by at a snail's pace. Maile felt her sanity slipping; a numbness that was not altogether displeasing enveloped her, and she suddenly didn't hurt anymore.

Maile felt as though she had been awake forever. A glance at the bracelet-watch that adorned her slender wrist told her she had been waiting for three hours. How much longer? a ragged voice screamed in her mind. Lord, how much more of this uncertainty could she stand?

Someone—Maile didn't know who—brought her a cup of coffee and sat with her for a few minutes, companionably quiet, but there in case Maile wanted to talk.

And then Jake was there, striding forward determinedly, his face set, a grayness shadowing his upper lip. Even before he spoke, his eyes had carefully searched her for injuries from head to toe.

"Maile! Oh, God, darling, I thought—" Bending, he crushed her to him in a fierce embrace, lifting her completely off the floor. "I didn't know what to think when that damn cop you sent after me said that you needed me in the hospital. I drove like a maniac to get to you." He rained tiny kisses of relief over her face, his arms tightening around her as though he were afraid that, if he relaxed his hold on her, she would slip out of his arms—vanish, perhaps. Maile smiled with relief as his mouth came down softly on hers.

Her relief was short-lived, and turned bittersweet as her eyes went over his shoulder to the big-eyed blonde standing at the door into the waiting room. Even if he had thought she was dying, he had not taken the time to dump his little lovebird. Maile stiffened in his arms and glared at Janice.

Sensing her withdrawal from him, Jake relaxed his hold on her. Maile touched the floor, and immediately started to struggle out of his arms.

"Maile, what's wrong?" Eyes clouded with concern roamed over her grim expression; his brows drew together in puzzlement.

"It's David. He's been hurt, Jake." She felt his arms tighten around her, hurtfully, and she winced. "It happened when he took off in my car. . . ." She let her voice trail off to an unhappy silence, knowing he, too, was thinking of the reason David had taken off like a bat out of hell.

"Damn him!" he hissed, shaking his head. Immediately his arms dropped away from her, and he turned away, muttering curses in an angry voice.

Maile stared at him in confusion. Why was he so angry? My God, didn't he care that the poor kid was in there, fighting for his very life? Dazed, she reached up a hand and smoothed back her hair.

Reaction set in slowly; anger slipped past her numbness, making her tremble.

181

"Oh, you're great!" she cried furiously, glaring up at Jake. "What the hell's the matter with you, Jake? Don't you care?" He turned, a dazed expression in his eyes. Too angry to see how he was suffering, Maile continued in a voice tight with contempt. "The poor kid might be dying, and all you can think is to curse his stupidity. And if he should . . . d-die, you'll probably be angry be-be-*because*"—she landed on the word, hard, angry with herself because she was crying—"because he didn't bother to ask you for permission!"

Jake blanched beneath his deep dark tan and reached out his hands to her, but she sidestepped, avoiding him as though he had some disease she was afraid of catching. She turned her back to him, letting her tears fall at will. What did she care now who saw her crying?

Janice took a step toward Jake, changed her mind, and walked to stand behind Maile.

"I know you're hurt, Maile, and you can't see anyone's point but your own." She took a deep breath, and placed her hand on Maile's shoulder. "But just look at Jake, Maile. He's suffering.

"Men don't have it easy like we do, Maile. They can't always cry on the outside. But it doesn't mean that they don't hurt. Jake loves his nephew, Maile." She took a deep breath, expelling it in a sigh. "And he loves *you*."

Maile shrugged off the hand on her shoulder. She stared fixedly at the night traffic below, crawling slowly northward. She wished she could be in their midst; she wished she weren't a part of this little drama here.

At last she turned, catching Jake unawares. It tore her insides to see that hopeless look on such a strong person.

"Jake?"

With a groan Jake moved across the room to her; he

enfolded her in his arms, burying his head in the crook between her neck and shoulder. Maile felt a great shudder travel over that masculine body, and felt a constriction in her throat.

"I'm sorry, Jake." Hand visibly shaking, she began to smooth down the rumpled black hair that had been raked by angry, impatient fingers. "I'm so sorry. . . ." He nodded against her neck. He understood. The tightening of his arms around her let her know that he understood; perhaps he was even telling her that he, too, was sorry. Maile hugged him hard.

The doctor came toward them, his step weary, his expression bland, giving Maile no clue to what he had come to tell them. She stiffened in Jake's arms, and immediately Jake lifted his head. Dazedly he stared into her eyes, his brow furrowed with confusion.

"Maile?"

"The doctor, Jake."

Jake tensed, and the hand that remained on her hip doubled into a fist. Maile stood beside him, rigid with fear.

She opened her mouth, but nothing came out. Nervously she cleared her throat and tried again. "Doctor, how is he?"

"Your nephew's going to be all right, Mrs. Weston," the doctor replied, giving her a tired smile. "He's in the ICU now, and you can see him for a moment. But only for a moment," he cautioned. He glanced up at Jake, his brow wrinkling. "I take it you are the boy's uncle?" Jake nodded slowly, and the doctor continued. "Well, sir, you may see him after a while. For now, the boy wants only to see his aunt. . . ."

Maile cringed. She knew Jake was hurt because his nephew had not immediately asked to see him. "Doctor,

183

uh, before his accident, he was upset because he thought we were not getting along. . . . If he could see us together, however briefly, it might help, don't you agree?"

The doctor smiled. "Perhaps. It can't hurt, if you promise you'll stay only for a moment." He showed them the way to the Intensive Care Unit, then left them.

Hands clasped tightly together, Maile and Jake stood at the door, for a moment hesitant to proceed. Then Maile straightened, standing on her toes to speak into the intercom, and announced that she was there to see Arthur Muccia. The faceless voice on the other end announced that the door was open, and she could proceed—quietly.

The nurse standing guard over her patients came quickly to the door when she saw there were two of them, and in a hushed, urgent voice told Jake that he would have to wait outside.

"No," Maile whispered, clinging to Jake's hand. "The doctor said it was all right for him to come in for a moment."

Grudgingly the nurse stepped aside, and they went into the room. They moved cautiously forward, Maile holding her breath as she peered through the semidarkness to find David. And in the next moment she was wishing she had not seen him there on the bed. He was so pale, so foreign-looking. Her heart cringed with hurt for him.

"David," she whispered, leaning down, peering into his face. "It's Maile, honey."

His hand moved. Maile quickly freed her hand from Jake's and took David's hand in both of hers. His fingers tried to tighten around her thumb, but he was too weak. Trembling lips managed a smile, although his eyes remained closed.

"Jake's here too," she said, and for a moment held her

breath as pain flitted across his face. But then his other hand moved, his fingers managing somehow to form a V for peace. A smile briefly lightened his pale features.

It was not even a minute later that the nurse came to shoo them away from David's side. They left quietly, though reluctantly.

Outside in the corridor Maile had to squint again to shade her eyes against the brightness. She felt Jake's arm snake around her waist and she leaned tiredly against him.

"I'm taking you home," he said decisively. "You're dead on your feet."

Maile was not in an argumentative frame of mind, but there was something they needed to clear up before she would go very far with him.

"Aren't you forgetting about Janice?"

"No. But you should—at least until you've had some sleep and are in a better frame of mind than when I last saw you." His tone was noncommittal, and it grated on her already frayed nerves.

"I'm tired, Jake," she whispered, and moved away from him. "Now that I know David's going to be all right, I think—"

"His name is *Arthur*," Jake said, his voice quiet but emphatic.

"I stand corrected," she mumbled. "However, now that I know he's going to be all right, there's no need for me to stay, or to come back. Good-bye, Jake."

Her footsteps echoed eerily in her ears as she walked away, feeling dejected and painfully lonely. He was letting her go! He was allowing her to walk out of the hospital and out of his life without even a lukewarm attempt to stop her. The tears overflowed her eyes and rolled down her tanned cheeks; she was too tired to fight them off.

Quickening her step, she rounded the corner, blurred eyes aimed fixedly on the elevator doors a few feet away.

The elevator was on its way up. Maile stood rigidly waiting for it to reach her floor and open its doors, trying not to even think that Jake had made no move to keep her with him. Not even a feeble attempt to come with me, she thought, feeling very sorry for herself.

Sighing deep from within her, she moved into the elevator and pressed the button for the main floor. He just doesn't care for me, that's all. And why should he? she questioned herself bitterly. She had given him what he wanted; what use was she to him now? He had had Janice standing in the sidelines the whole time, sweetly eager to satisfy all his male urges without being a trial to him with David—like *she* was.

Unsteady legs carried her across the mezzanine, through the double glass doors, and out into the wintry night. A bright moon enjoying dominion of a cloudless sky threw dark golden beams over the parking lot, illuminating almost mockingly the battered little car she had had to drive to the hospital. An old rustic relic, she thought, forcing a little smile to her trembling lips. She and it belonged together; they were both well used, but still pretty serviceable. . . .

She opened the door and climbed in, and for a moment just sat there staring over the steering wheel. A hand went up to her neck, and she massaged her tired muscles while rotating her head to ease some of the tension out of her shoulders. It had been a long, long day.

Maile backed slowly out of her parking slot, then shifted into first gear and drove slowly toward the exit. Shifting up another gear, she went out of the parking lot, easing her car into the light flow of traffic leaving the city.

Wearily keeping her eyes fixed on the center line of the pavement, she negotiated her way home, carelessly unaware of the traffic whizzing past her. A numbness had settled in again, and she was able to avoid getting into trouble along the way only because she was a good driver who automatically did all the right things.

Had she left her porch light on? She couldn't remember; but she was grateful for its being on, considering it a small measure of welcome. This was something familiar; it nagged some sort of feeling into her body.

"Now, I *know* I didn't leave my door unlocked," she whispered musingly after trying to unlock the door and finding it already unlocked. Very cautiously she turned the knob and opened the door. Her living room was dark, but there was a light in her kitchen—and the unmistakable smell of fresh coffee brewing.

"Maile?" Jake's voice preceded him into the room. "I've got coffee brewing." He strode forward almost hesitantly, a smile twitching the corners of his mouth.

"No, don't go, Maile," he cautioned in a voice that made her immediately freeze, though every nerve end tingled with a crazy desire to run. "You wouldn't get very far," he added in a tone that was almost amused.

"No. I'm too tired to run, Jake," she admitted wearily and stepped farther into the living room. Too tired to run; too tired to fight him, she thought as he covered the distance between them with a few easy strides.

"I know what you need, Maile. It's what I need, too, but for now, let me just hold you, honey." His arms went around her, tenderly, almost as though he were afraid she would hurt if he tightened his hold on her. His arms were warm; they had all the power to crush her breath from her, but they were almost unbelievably gentle.

Feeling slowly crept through her, along with a pleasant warmth. Maile nuzzled her cheek against the soft silk of the multicolored shirt that stretched tautly across a great expanse of chest.

"And what is it you think I need, Jake?" she asked, a trifle cynically.

Laughing softly, he tilted her face up to his with two fingers under her chin. "You *know* exactly what I meant, baby. And you also know that I'm right," he added in a confident tone just a shade short of being arrogant.

Swiftly Maile's face suffused with color. "You think sex is a cure for everything, don't you?" she challenged dryly, lips trembling with a sudden urge to be kissed.

"Well, maybe not for *everything*. . . ." His tone was doubtful.

Arrogant as always, she thought, but instead of being angry, she smiled and, lifting her chin fractionally, she escaped his fingers.

"You're not going anywhere, lady," he said when Maile started away from his arms. "I kinda like where you are, and for once, you're quiet. A pleasant change."

Frowning, Maile looked up at him and started to upbraid him, but he told her quietly to shut up, and she did. His tone was sober, and his expression almost frighteningly grave.

"I heard what the doctor called you. . . ."

Oh, boy, now he's going to tell me that I had no right to do what I did, regardless of the fact that if I hadn't, his nephew might've died, she thought, her heart sinking to her toes.

"And?" she quaked, forcing herself to meet his eyes.

"And I kinda liked the sound of it. Mrs. Weston . . . Maile Weston. It has a nice ring to it," he said in a drawling voice. "So what do you think? Wanna marry me before the cops come after you for giving a fraudulent name to the hospital?" His eyes twinkled with mischief.

"Is that a proposal, Jake?" Her voice was tight; the words drawn forcibly past the lump of fear in her chest.

"If it isn't, Maile, it's the closest I'm ever going to come to one." Smiling, he cupped his large hand around her chin, lifting her face to kiss her. "You know me—I'm so much better at propositions."

Maile sagged against him. "You're impossible, Jake Weston!" she cried, lifting her face for another kiss. "And I just don't know what I'm going to do with you!"

"You can marry me, for one. And, for another . . ." Bending swiftly, he scooped her up into his arms and marched into her bedroom.

"What do you think you're doing?" she shrieked, fully aware of what he was doing. Still, perversely, she demanded he take her into the kitchen. She wanted to talk; she wanted to hear him say that he loved her and *wanted* to marry her. She wasn't quite ready to accept that half-baked proposal.

But Jake was not going to give her a chance to fight him off. Crawling across the bed on his knees, he deposited her on the center of the bed, hurriedly undressed, and then he lay down beside her.

"What does it look like I'm doing, love?" he taunted softly while his hands worked furiously at the buttons on her blouse. "I thought by now you wouldn't need to be *told.*"

Maile stretched languorously against him, "like a seductive kitten," said Jake, and she grinned. "I *want* to be told," she insisted, adopting a furious look.

Immediately his hands stopped what they were doing,

189

and though she missed his caresses, she was stubbornly set on hearing the words.

"I *love* you, Maile, and I've been a chump not to ask you before to be my wife.

"You see, darling, I fancied myself in love once before with a woman who came on sweet and innocent, quite like you. She, too, belonged to someone else—not like you, Maile. I know now that if Mike Sloan had not died, I would never have stood a chance with you."

"Go on," she urged thickly, wishing he would hurry through whatever it was he had to say.

"I promised myself, after that, that I would never let another woman do that to me. I swore I would take what they could give me and move on, heart-whole and unscathed.

"But if you don't marry me, Maile, I won't leave that way. You'll always have a large part of me. . . ." His voice had softened to a whisper that was almost inaudible.

"I don't want just a part of you, Jake," Maile told him, her voice tight with emotion. "I want all of you. But if you're not ready to give me all of you, then, no, I won't marry you."

"Dear God," he moaned. "You've had all of me for so long, honey. I was just too dense to realize it." Then his mouth crushed hers, his hands began to move persuasively over her, molding the softness of her pliant body to the throbbing masculine length of his.

"Oh, Jake. . ." she breathed.

"Oh, Jake, what?" he prompted.

Maile sighed with contentment as his hand went down to caress her thigh and then moved up to skim her hips and taut stomach.

"I love you, Jake," she murmured, parting her lips

beneath his mouth that moved with deliberate slowness over hers.

"And I love you, Maile." His hands became torches that seared her skin with loving caresses as they traveled at their leisure over her body, easing her out of her clothes, igniting the flames of passion in them both. Maile moaned; she sought to deepen his kiss, arching her body beneath the sinewy one that loomed above her.

"As soon as Arthur is well enough to stand up with me, we're going to get married," he murmured, moving slightly away from her. He smiled. "And for a prewedding present, I am going to take you to Canada and let you witness the arrest of that embezzling little bitch that has caused us all so much trouble.

"Then, afterward, we can come back to Seattle—"

Maile reached up to grab him, to pull him down to her again. Placing caressing fingers across his sensuous mouth, she stifled whatever protest the man was going to make, chuckling softly as she snaked her arms around his neck to hold his face in place while she kissed him.

"Wanton!" Jake jeered lovingly, his mouth lowering deliciously over hers.

"Yeah, but you love it," she teased, smiling beneath his mouth. She sighed with contentment. And as he moved over her she knew without a doubt that whatever stormy days their future held—and to be sure, with their temperaments, there would be plenty—their love would carry them through.